THE SUICIDE
LETTERS OF
JACK MONROE

Also by Mary Maurice

Fruit Loops the Serial Killer
Burtrum Lee
The Suicide Letters of Jack Monroe

THE SUICIDE LETTERS OF JACK MONROE

By

Mary Maurice

Keep on bookin'!
Mary M Maurice

SILVER
LEAF
BOOKS

HOLLISTON, MASSACHUSETTS

THE SUICIDE LETTERS OF JACK MONROE

Copyright © 2018 by Mary Maurice

Cover Art by Joel Nakamura.

First printing September 2018
10 9 8 7 6 5 4 3 2 1

ISBN # 978-1-60975-237-8
ISBN (eBook) # 978-1-60975-238-5
LCCN # 2018946450

Silver Leaf Books, LLC
P.O. Box 6460
Holliston, MA 01746
+1-888-823-6450

Visit our web site at www.SilverLeafBooks.com

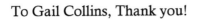

To Gail Collins, Thank you!

THE SUICIDE
LETTERS OF
JACK MONROE

JULY

Dear Susan,

I have nothing against suicide. I just hope it's for the right reasons.

There's been no word from you since my arrival here in Santa Fe, and I'm wondering how you are. As you know, I came to the Southwest to try to talk you out of going through with your plans—per your request—and I'd hoped to have seen you by now.

I understand, though. Your life is in an upheaval, and I'm sure you don't know which way is up or down, and believe me, sister, I know what you're going through. I wouldn't be here right now had it not been for the saving grace of something unknown.

Anywho, I won't get into that right now!

I don't know how you can stand this dry, hot air. I can barely breathe, and every time I do, I inhale dust. My tongue is all white and cracked, like dried curdled milk. Give me a stale Oreo, and I'd have a snack.

And the architecture! What's with the mud huts? I don't get it. Personally, I'll take the dusty, crime filled streets of Detroit; at least there's some action there. Maybe that's part of the problem. You need a change of venue. A new environment. A place where your blood can start flowing again, and you can take in some oxygen.

Now, don't get me wrong. I'm not suggesting you move back to Michigan. I'm just saying maybe your senses need a different scene.

Guess I'm not giving Santa Fe a fair chance; I've only been in this town a few days. Maybe the right vibe just has to set in. After all, some locals say this place is magical, that there's a huge crystal right below the foundation of the city. From way back when, guess it began to form right after all the volcanoes blew up. Believe what you must!

I think with the two of us working on this problem, we can brainstorm and figure out what you should do with your life. Then you can decide whether or not you want to end it.

Believe me Susan, as I said before, since I opened my business, *Suicide Letters by Jack Monroe*, I've lost no clients; few though there were. Plus, you have to remember it was you who contacted me; so deep down, in some hidden way, you must want my help.

I'm roasting as the hot Southwest sun rises over my shoulder, streaming into the side of my eye. The brightness blinds me for a moment. I see silver sparkles dancing against a black setting, kind of like a bad reel-to-reel, flickering like a strobe light. I glimpse pictures of myself as a child, young and fearful. Wondering about the moment death gives birth to finality. Did I know then what I don't know now?

Maybe!

Susan, did I ever tell you about my first client? Probably, but here goes again.

I had just started an advertisement in this rag magazine called "The Dank, Dark & Disgusting." The clip read: *Need help writing the perfect suicide letter? At a loss for words? Contact Jack Monroe , CEO of Suicide Letters by Jack Monroe. P.O. Box 753, Hazel Park, MI 48030. All inquiries answered.*

At first I didn't get any responses. I'm sure people must have thought I was nuts. But then this young girl wrote to me, describing how she was depressed after her boyfriend dumped her when he found out she was pregnant. She rushed into an abortion, regretting the procedure immediately. Her grief was unbearable. All she wanted to do was kill herself. Quickly!

Jessica (not her real name) was barely eighteen, and her despair was heart wrenching. I tell you, Susan, I was nervous. I knew if I said the wrong thing, wrote the wrong words, she'd murder herself for sure, that's how determined she was.

Time was of the essence, so one dim night as I sat quietly in my kitchen, head bent over a yellow legal pad, blue pen in hand, I composed her suicide letter.

It went something like this:

> *Dear Mom and Dad,*
>
> *First and foremost, I want to apologize for all the hurt and pain I've caused you in my short lifetime. Mom, Dad, it isn't your fault, I just can't stand the thought of living with this feeling of regret and dread. I assassinated my baby! How can I go on?*
>
> *I can hear you now, Dad, if I was there, we'd be talking, you telling me what a wonderful young woman I am, and this is just a mistake, one of those life lessons a person needs to learn in order to gain character. And Mom, your loving, but sorrowful eyes, welling up in fearful tears for the little girl you lost, and the tainted daughter who now stands before you. You'd tell me not to worry, that I can always have more children when I meet the right guy, and then I'll know what true love is all about.*

And of course you're right. Then the two of you will try to comfort me by saying, "tomorrow is another day." No truer words can be spoken. But today it's hard to face the beautiful dawn sky; the pale purple horizon with its mirrored moon setting in the west, while the sun ascends into the mellow morning.

Please forgive me!

Your Loving Daughter,
Jessica

I don't know what happened, but she decided not to take her life. Now honestly, Susan, do you see anything special about this letter that would make Jessica change her mind? I think seeing the words in print, really brought it home; opened the door to the reality of what she was truly planning. Gave her a sneak-peak at how she would ruin the lives of the people she loves.

All I know is she's alive today, and has two beautiful little girls.

Not to toot my own horn, but I feel it's important to let you know I'm good at what I do. And if you would just give me a chance, I think I could really help. Trust me when I tell you, though, it won't be all roses and vanilla ice cream. This subject is very delicate and fragile, filled with hidden emotions, some which will scare us both. So, when you do decide to work with me, be prepared.

Okay, then, I'm going to sign off now. You know where I am, please call me or come by whenever convenient.

Your Friend,
Jack Monroe

Dear Susan,

I think I'm beginning to like this altitude. I know in my last letter I was pretty harsh about everything. But now that I'm starting to acclimate, I'm feeling better.

Everything is so laid back here, except for the bustling tourists cramming the streets.

Some of them are quite comical. Looking so lost and out of sorts—not sure what is where, or where is what. Makes me chuckle! I'm sure there have been times when I've gotten those same looks and expressions. I wonder what shmuck was laughing at me.

I worry sometimes that my coming here might be pushing you away from me. Scaring you from my assistance. And that's all I want to do, Susan, is be there for you. Believe me when I tell you, there are no other motives behind my intentions.

At times I think the reason why you don't contact me is because you know I might change your mind, and right now you don't want that. Okay, fine, I'll just keep writing. And if you don't care enough to check out my advice, then just throw my letters away. Maybe one day, though, I'll annoy you to the point where you'll call me just to tell me to leave you alone. At least then I'll know you're still alive!

So, I guess in a way, I do have reasons behind my actions.

Do you know what I wish? That you would just tell me what has brought you to this place. Is it a man? A woman? Your family, or the way you look? Are you lonely, depressed, just out of whack?

There has to be a why. All we have to do is tap into it, and then we can fix the problem.

See how easy this is going to be?

Plus, my fees are reasonable!

The one thing we don't want to do is keep ourselves isolated. In my opinion, isolation feeds our fears, torments those demons residing within. We need to be out and about, communing with nature. Oh, and throw in some people; they give us the re-assurance that, *no*, we are not alone. That, in itself, should make you start feeling better!

Hopefully down the line, these letters will have an impact on both of us, and we can better our lives because of them.

Your Friend,
Jack Monroe

Dear Susan,

A surprise rain today. The locals rejoice, tourists pout. Apparently the skies have been dry as a bone for the past few months, and the continuous ninety-degree weather is heating up everyone's nerves to the sizzling point.

Sitting here and smelling the spiciness of the wet rain makes me feel a little melancholy. Not quite sad, but reserved. It's as if the absent sun and the memory— revealing rain, are transporting me back to a time and place I'd hoped I would never think of again. But that's not how the brain works, is it? Try to think happy, and inevitably the pain starts seeping back in.

I think it's just a crease in time.

I wouldn't mind finding a golf course somewhere close by. Maybe hit a few balls... release some of this tension nestled in my joints. Suppose I could try to stretch here, in my room, but everything's so cramped, yet empty. Kind of what you must be feeling, I'd think. But that's neither here nor there. Who am I to tell you what you're feeling? Most of the time I'm unsure about my own emotions.

I told you in a previous letter about how Mom died, right? I was twelve—remember—and had just come home from school. A wing-tipped red ambulance was parked in front of my house, its bubble gum siren whirling. It was a hot, early November day. The temperature set a new record for the greater Detroit area.

There was an awful smell too, one I'll never forget. All those moist, decaying leaves, and the steamy vapors rising, as the sun beat down on the rotting foliage. The air smelled of death-sweet, dark and wet.

My skin turned clammy. My Levi jeans felt heavy around my waist as I trudged past the black and white police car and into my house, unnoticed, as though I were invisible.

I moved in a daze to the back bedroom where Mom used to sleep. Peering around the corner, I saw her small white, delicate hand hanging over the side of the bed, like a deflated balloon.

I heard my name being screamed, but it was far off, somewhere in a different canyon, where the valley was lush with green vegetation. My own voice broke the silence as I screeched, "*Mom!*" I plunged toward her. My Uncle Bob swooped me up into his arms and carried me away.

That was it. I never saw her again. I wasn't allowed to go to the funeral. I was too young, they said. It wasn't until years later that I found out the truth about her death. They'd told me she had fallen and hit her head on the dresser and died. Internal brain hemorrhage, or something like that. Finally, more out of spite than anything, Dad told me the truth. It wasn't a brain-bleed at all, but an overdose. He claimed it was my fault Mom had killed herself. Said I was too much of a damned brat, and she just couldn't take it anymore. I didn't believe him, though. Not for a moment. I knew how much Mom loved me.

There was no note found, so I never knew the real reasons for her suicide. All I know is, Dad continued to blame me 'til the day he died. I suppose that's part of the reason why I decided to start this suicide letter business, so people would know the reasons for the victim's actions, and wouldn't blame themselves for the rest of their lives.

I wish I could've written one for Mom.

Anywho!

Still, if I live in the past, I'll never get anywhere. I loved Mom, and for whatever reasons she did what she did, I'm sure she thought them justified. I find them selfish.

Do you believe I've written this whole letter without a mistake! Did you know that through all of Anais Nin's hand written diaries, there's not one error. They're all perfectly scribed. And she had about sixty-nine journals, or something like that. Can you imagine?

Just a little bit of trivia.

When I first started my enterprise, I'd thought about taking a course in letter writing or composition. Try to be professional about this new venture I was entering. But then after a few classes I saw how impersonal they were becoming, and I decided to just go with my gut. Isn't that the best way?

Here I go babbling again. Much ado about nothing!

My mind is getting sleepy. I'm not totally accustomed to the altitude yet. I'll take a little nap and then mail this. Please write, let me know how you are.

Your Friend,
Jack Monroe

Dear Susan,

I'm sweltering! I don't know how much longer I can take it in this hellhole. There's nothing here. Everything's dirty and dusty, even the people are all beginning to look the same. Their faces expressionless, eyes void of sparkle. It's as though I were walking amongst the living dead. Today, in the Land of Enchantment, I'm not very enchanted.

I can't believe you've stayed this long. What's it been, six months now? I don't know how you can stand it. Maybe one of the reasons *why* you want to kill yourself is because you live here!

Think about it!

I'm sorry, I didn't mean that. I'm just wound a little tighter than normal. Give me a minute and let me catch my breath. I can feel the frustration of not hearing from you burn through me. I don't understand why you won't contact me. Weren't you the one who asked me to come to Santa Fe because you needed help? Well?

I'm beginning to believe I'm making a mistake being here. While I'm spending this time getting nowhere with you, I could be helping someone else. Somebody who really wants and needs my services. I'm beginning to think you're just messing with me, and I don't like it.

Trust me when I say I'm not putting the whole blame on you. It's partly my fault. I should never have met with you. I knew when I went against rule number one—never meet a client in person—that I was heading down a steep slope. Normally, I hold my communications to snail mail, no physical contact at all. Not even their voices. So you can understand why it was so unusual for me to rendezvous with you in person.

There was just some unexplained reason, though. Maybe I needed to see what kind of woman you truly are, and answer the question gnawing at me, *why*?

I'm beginning to regret my breaking protocol.

You really should reconsider going to a doctor, Susan. Get a professional opinion. Could be you're just experiencing a chemical imbalance. Happens all of the time to people. Maybe all you need to do is take some medication for a while till everything evens out.

I'll chip in for the expenses, so don't worry about the money.

Think about it, okay?

I'm kind of hungry, but not really. I think I'll wait and get food later. I remember when I was younger, my grandfather once said to me I should eat when I can, not just when I'm hungry. While sitting in his orange straight back chair, dying, his oxygen mask strapped onto his gaunt face, he'd dispense mumbled advice, while his glossy, bulbous eyes begged for one last Pall Mall.

A product of the depression era, he warned of coming economic bad times. "Soup lines," he'd hack, spraying the orb around himself. "Eat when you can," he'd suddenly blurt out.

My how things have changed. Now people don't give a second thought to wasting food.

Your Friend,
Jack Monroe

Dear Susan,

I've hit an all-time low. This trip isn't what I thought it would be. I'd hoped we would have met by now and, once we talked, you would come to your senses. Then we would fly back to Detroit, back to our homes, friends, and family, although I can't recall if you said your folks were still alive or not. I feel bad about forgetting something so important.

I don't understand why you are making things so complicated.

I had a dream last night that I am at my childhood home in Hazel Park, and in my old bedroom. I'd put some towels out to dry, beach towels I believe, striped with colorful reds, blues, and purples, exuding summer fun. I hang them over the balcony railing on the roof, even though there is nothing like that on the house I grew up in and still reside at. I step out onto the porch and the planks are old and gray, some bending like bows in the middle. I feel sad, like an important moment has passed me by and I missed it.

I wonder what the instant was, and would I recognize the time if it came around again?

Do you know what I want to do, Susan? I want to celebrate life for the beauty it possesses. Drink in the magnificent marvels surrounding us. I bet that would make you feel better.

I suddenly feel a headache inching its way into my head. It's been a long time since one has occurred. I'd better sign off now, turn off the lights, and lie down, before it turns into a mind bomb.

Please, Susan, call me or drop a note. I really need to hear from you!

Your Friend,
Jack Monroe

Dear Susan,

This place is something else. There I was, standing in the plaza watching the sun set into these dark lavender clouds framing the salmon sky, when all of a sudden I hear this loud clap of thunder and it starts to pour. I had no defense, no place to run, nothing to cover myself with. By the time the rains had stopped some minutes later, I was soaked to the bone.

Now, I sit in my room shivering and wondering if I'll ever get warm again.

Wasn't that Job's frequent lament, Susan? "Woe unto me!"

I stare out the window, and see ominous thunderheads shrouding the mountains, weakening into sheer white mist floating over the green hills. Water-dogs, I believe they're nick-named. It makes my heart swell. All of a sudden my nerves tingle and I feel my breath running and hiding in my throat.

Have you ever felt that, Susan?

I'm tired. I've been listening to the news; it sucks. Nothing but people killing people and then killing themselves. What's the sense in that?

I'm sorry, I sound like a downer, and I am. I wish I had a happy story to tell you, a tale of my childhood, or an adventure of my young adulthood. But it seems my memories have taken a sabbatical. So, maybe I'll just sign off for now, and write again tomorrow. What else can I do?

Hope all is well!

Your Friend,
Jack Monroe

Dear Susan,

It was so weird today. I'm walking around and I hear this woman calling out to me as she quickly approaches. I was immobile as she came right up to my face and kissed me on the cheek, like we were best friends.

She started rambling on about how no one has seen or heard from me in a couple of weeks and asked if I was all right, and did I want to go have a cup of coffee and talk. It was quite awkward. I think she was on drugs or something, and hallucinating that I was someone else. Now how crazy is that?

I hastened away without a word, in spite of her pleas to come back following in my wake.

I tell you, people are nuts.

Hey, Susan, do you think maybe you're experiencing a metamorphosis?

Like the Phoenix is emerging from you, restructuring your whole being into something, or someone else?

There are times when that's how I feel.

It scares me, because I begin to question who I am.

Anywho!

I hear a chain saw. I guess the man who started to cut down the tree under my window yesterday is finishing up today. A slight breeze blows through the curtains, as a soft tweet of a Finch drifts through the blazing hot air.

No rain today.

My heart feels so heavy, Susan. Can you lighten it? I feel like you don't want to contact me because you're afraid I'll talk you out of your suicide plan. But I won't. I've decided to let you do whatever you want. Maybe I can help you do it right. After all, just think of how awful life would be if you screwed up. Ending up like a vegetable, maybe, or in a loony bin. There are things worse than death, you know.

Think about it!

Or we can just talk about candy-filled rainbows and rivers of salt water taffy, and all the fluffy things in life that make it worth living. We won't discuss anything depressing, just sunshine and sea-blue skies, I promise. And if anything, I am a man of my word.

Let me know.

Well, my dear Susan, I think I'm going to call it a night. I'm tired and hungry and am still a little freaked out from *that* mad woman.

Anyway!

Your Friend,
Jack Monroe

Dear Susan,

Damn dogs barking all morning, waking me up at around four. It drives me crazy. If there's one thing I don't like, it's my sleep being interrupted. Hard enough for me to nod off in the first place. Some people just don't have any consideration.

Reminds me of a Seinfeld episode where Elaine is kept up night after night by a barking hound. So she convinces Kramer to ditch the canine in the country. But the animal finds its way back, and continues to bark the night away. Hilarious!

I loved that show.

Now I'll be cranky all day, I'm afraid.

I certainly hope this isn't the day you decide to show up.

It's still very early, the dawn hasn't quite broken, but I can see the tangerine outline of the rising sun peek over the foothills. The air is cool and fresh, and even though I'm exhausted, I feel relaxed. Maybe I'll have to start getting up at daybreak from now on, it's such a beautiful and peaceful time.

When do you usually roll out of bed, Susan?

Anyway, I'm just babbling on, again. Forgive me. The coffee must be hitting.

I think I'm going to drive up to Taos this morning and check out the Rio Grande Gorge Bridge. I hear it's pretty amazing. I have a little case of vertigo, so I don't know how close I'll get to the rail. But I'm sure it's a spectacular sight even from a distance.

You know, Susan, they say this area of New Mexico

used to be an ocean, and we're living on the sea's floor. I've seen strange formations made millions of years ago by the water; frozen sand sculptures, some reminding me of animals dried solid in time. I'm mesmerized. I feel so small compared to the vastness of the land.

It's humbling.

Poor people! Don't you think, Susan? They all work so hard for things of no real consequence, suffering and striving their whole existence for possessions they just leave behind anyway. And when they do get what they want, they always want more. And when they don't have what they want, they're miserable.

So, I'm trying not to want anything. Just take what life has to give me, what I deserve. Now, don't get me wrong. I'm not saying I'm going to lie down and do nothing. Of course I'll do something, and that is to work on my spiritual self. Don't you think by getting in touch with that part of your being, you'll find peace, and then everything you deserve will come your way?

I hope I'm not sounding too holy roller for you. That's not where I'm coming from. I just think if people would relax and not stress over things they really shouldn't have or need in the first place, the world would be a better place.

I was a blue-collar working man for eighteen years. Can you imagine? Running machinery at this small factory that made the little switches for car door lights. Millions of them. It was not a very exciting career. One I don't want to experience again.

Then, after my debilitating injury, I ventured into the suicide letter writing business and here I am today. Still living in the same house I grew up in as a kid. Never left. Stayed there with Dad after Mom's death. I just couldn't leave him alone in his condition. He never really recovered from her suicide. So, I basically was raised in a non-emotional environment, never knowing what it was like to be truly loved.

Oh woe unto me!

Anywho!

Did you know a butterfly's body temperature has to be 60 degrees before it can fly?

See, that's why they sunbathe on walls!

Adieu for now, my dearest Susan. I'll write soon!

Your Friend,
Jack Monroe

Dear Susan,

The most terrible thing has happened. After I finished writing you the last letter, I decided to go down and take a swim in the hotel pool. Well, when I got there, a small group of people were milling around outside the entrance to the grotto. I was a little disappointed because I was hoping to have the place to myself. No one was entering, though. I edged closer, trying to slip through them, when a man grabbed my arm and asked me where I was going.

Startled, I muttered "I'd like to go for a swim." He released me and said the patio was closed. "Why?" I asked. He said a little girl had just drowned.

I could feel the blood drain from my face as I shuffled away. How could something so bad happen on such a nice day? See, it's the demon. The one always lurking around, never allowing true happiness to enter your life. I know him personally.

Those poor parents, having to live with the guilt of losing their daughter by unwatchful eyes.

I banged against brown/gray walls in my hastened escape, trying desperately to reach my room. I whipped in, slamming the empty door behind my shadow. Sobs trembled through me. I can't stop weeping. I'm drained. Feels like Mom's suicide all over again.

Have been in bed now for three days.

I never made it to the Gorge!

Is this an ominous sign?

Life is sad, don't you think, Susan? I mean, sure there are those days with perfect moments, the ones you wish would last forever. The times making you believe, if only for an instant, that all is right with the world.

I experienced a similar sensation just the other day as I hiked up to the Cross of the Martyrs. You know, the area dedicated to some war and its dead soldiers. Anyhow, there's a panoramic view from up there. All around me, these majestic mountains rise and meet the sky. Fortresses of molten rock. I'd never experienced anything like it. My body became transformed as though my mind was being touched. My heart went weightless.

I felt like I was Maria in the Sound of Music twirling around on the grassy knoll.

I'm cold, I look down at my hairy legs, brown-gray bristles map the flaky skin. No wonder I don't wear shorts. If I can't stand the sight of my own legs, how could anyone else?

Do you want to know which way of dying I fear most? Probably not, but I'll tell you anyway. My greatest fear is of being burned alive in a fire. I don't think I would handle that very well. Waking up with a blaze surrounding you, and you're so disoriented you can't find your way out. That's what I'm afraid of!

What about you? What's your biggest fear? Do you have one? I'm sure you do. I believe the general public dreads death. Maybe it's not the actual dying, but the factor of the unknown. Where do we go? I speculate that the truth is being kept secret because the other side is so cool everyone would want to go there. And who would be left to slave away? I guess I shouldn't be saying this to someone who's contemplating suicide, should I?

Although, I suppose once you get over the fear of dying, it's gotta be a lot easier to take your own life. After all, it's not about anyone else but yourself, right? No one else matters in your life, isn't that true, Susan?

The fear of death keeps us from living our true lives. It…

Oh, skip it! I'm tired of talking about such morbid subjects.

Oh, Susan, I miss you. I wish you would just let me know you're all right. That's all. If you don't want to talk to me, I understand. You're going through a lot, but at least let me know you're still alive. Okay? Surely that's not too much to ask!

I've decided after all of this is said and done, I'm going to take a little trip to Jamaica. Hang out on the beach for a couple of months, maybe smoke some ganja, or whatever they call it. Not write any more letters for a while. I can feel it starting to get to me. But I promise I'll put my full efforts and energies into this mission with you.

Don't worry.

Did I ever tell you about the time I wanted to join the army? This was after I quit college. Well, I went to enlist, but I didn't get in. There was an issue about something not being quite right somewhere. I think they didn't like the looks of me. After all, I have been a little anemic my whole life.

Well, Susan, another end to another letter. I need a shower. I just caught a whiff of myself, and I'm pretty ripe. Take care!

Your Friend,
Jack Monroe

Dear Susan,

Bored by this interminable waiting, I decided to take a stroll to the plaza, and am sitting here now as I write this. Tourists mill around. A kind of quiet seizes the air as the streets are blocked off from cars because of the pedestrian traffic. It's nice, but for how long? I need the chaos of the city, the tall, glass-ridden buildings standing inanimate around me, people rudely rushing past, knocking against each other as if we were in a game of bumper bodies.

That's my thing!

I wish I could think of a joke to tell you, but I have trouble recalling them. Right before Dad died, he couldn't remember anything. I suppose that's a good thing. Then, you don't die regretting the bad memories and cursing the happy times!

Don't you think?

Well, my Dear Sweet, I think I'm going to go back to my hotel room, grab a bite and relax for the rest of the day. I'm starting to feel better, a little lighter.

Thank you!

Your Friend,
Jack Monroe

Dear Susan,

I wish I were at Tiger Stadium right now, cheering on the Tigers. I love baseball!

Remember in my last letter when I said I was starting to feel better, a little lighter, or something in that manner. Well, by golly, the sensation is sticking. Today, I'm a brand new man. Maybe it's because the air has cooled down and I feel a sensation of nostalgia. Whatever it is, I hope the mood stays.

I keep reliving our meeting and how depressed you were. Your listless affect, and the sardonic tone of your voice as you spewed regurgitated words at me. It didn't seem like you were very interested in what I had to offer; that's why I was a little baffled when I received your letter asking me to come to Santa Fe.

Wait, let me go get it, and I'll quote you direct.

Damn-it, I can't find the note. I must've left it on my desk back in Detroit. Anyway, I'm sure you know what you wrote. The desperation in your words. Even though there was still no explanation as to why you wished to proceed.

So, what happened? I thought you had reconsidered your plans when you told me you didn't think you'd need my services.

Why the change of heart?

Did your girlfriend leave you?

Did you get fired?

Did you find out you had a terminal disease?

Come on, Susan, tell me. I'm getting tired of playing these games. Maybe, just maybe, I'm going to stop writing you altogether. Then, where will you be?

Alone!

See, look what happens. I start thinking of you and my emotions turn dark. Why is this? What am I doing to myself? I feel like I've been in a pond too long, but I don't want to get out because the air has turned cool. So, I sit in tepid water watching the setting sun in the sky steal the heat of the day away. Ripples of still water circle me like covered wagons. The posse has found me, there's no escape.

I still don't want to get out, even though my skin chills with goose-bumps.

I'm now at *Monsignor Patrick Smith Park* up on Alameda, by Canyon Road. It's a beautiful lush field with trees and soccer nets. A game is in progress as I sit here picking up where I left off with the letter from earlier.

I'm sorry, I didn't mean to get so harsh. It's just sometimes I get really frustrated, you know?

I can smell the grass, bringing me home. The scent should be an incense stick, or a color in a box of crayons. *Green Grass.* It'd be a million-dollar seller. Ah, who needs money. I tell ya, if I didn't have bills, I wouldn't charge for my services. Wouldn't that be nice? If humans just exchanged their natural gifts with each other, then no one would have to labor. The farmer can give me potatoes, and I can keep his daughter from committing suicide.

Can't think of a fairer deal.

Do I sound a little Lenin-Marxist? Talk about two guys who had the right concept, in a way.

Anywho, I'm breeching a practice of never discussing

politics with my clients.

I seem to be breaking a lot of rules when it comes to you.

Santa Fe is beginning to grow on me, although I feel sorry for the City Different. The exploitation of its beauty and native population is despicable in my eyes. Progress has moved in and is changing this enchanting town into just another tourist attraction. I suppose money has to come from somewhere.

I watch the yellow/green poplars sway in the cool evening breezes. The chilling sun sparkles on them, turning their leaves to glitter from far away. My stomach is gurgling, again, a never ending sound of rolling gases.

I need a *Tums*!

Your Friend,
Jack Monroe

Dear Susan,

Oh, my gosh, oh, my gosh, it's three-thirty in the morning and I just awoke from the weirdest dream. You were in it. *We are at this B&B, but I'm not sure where the inn is located. As I look out the window I see an undistinguishable mountain range in the distance. I go downstairs to talk to the keeper whose name is Rose. She is an elderly woman who should have retired years ago. She insists she'll take me for a drive so I can figure out where I am. I have no idea where you are. As we're driving, Rose, announces we are near Santa Rosa. Suddenly, she veers off into a field and heads toward a frozen river, even though it's summer. I'm screaming at her that we are about to drive into the rapids, but she pays no heed to my warnings and proceeds to plow forward. At first we aren't sinking. But then as we get nearer to the opposite bank, the car begins to submerge. I tell Rose to unbuckle her seatbelt, and grabbing her, I drag her frail,-bony body through my window and into the freezing water. We swim to shore and even though the river is ice, I'm not cold. The water is deep sea blue, with tiny glaciers floating on top of it, like the Artic. I am disturbed and comforted at the same time by this lethal beauty. Suddenly, Rose slips from my grip, I watch as her head bobs down the falls. Feeling guilty that I can't save her, I glimpse your fearful eyes in her shallow face.*

Are you *Rose*?

Dawn will be here in a short while, and I haven't seen a sunrise in a long time. Maybe I should go for a walk, calm down, then come back and try to get some sleep. Wait, this can't be. As I look out my window, I see the already blazing sun crest the low hills. How did it get to be so late? I don't understand. Did I black out, lose consciousness? What happened?

Am I losing my mind? Oh, my God, I can feel that headache coming back. Inching slowly. I need to get back into bed, close the drapes, turn on the air conditioning. It's the only way I'll be able to survive this day.

The church bells chime six, they vibrate like an earthquake through my already vulnerable brain. I think this one is going to turn into a migraine.

Somebody, please help me!

Your Friend,
Jack Monroe

Dear Susan,

I'm confused! I don't know if the drowning child was real or a dream. There doesn't seem to be any sign of something so horrific happening around here, and I don't want to ask the desk clerk. He already thinks I'm nuts, and I'm sure he'll be glad to see me leave.

I just don't know!

Anyway, I went down to the pool, and there was no sign of any kind of tragedy.

Hasn't it been only a couple of days since the incident?

Did I imagine the whole thing?

The air around me feels dead, as though all life has been sucked out of it. There's a stillness that is unnerving.

Stifling!

I suppose that's one of the feelings of death. An airless, tight bubble where there are no thoughts, dreams, desires.

I can't breathe!

There's nothing!

My mind is tweaked right now, so I'm thinking about having a drink. But then, what good would that do? Just make matters worse, even though people believe booze helps them make it through troubled times.

Anywho!

The voices and noises rising from the street sound like a distant radio on some strange station. It adds to this surreal sensation I'm experiencing. I wonder if it has to do with the microwaves floating in the air? Electromagnetic spectrum. A rainbow that can affect your mind. At least that's what some people claim. They even say it can cause cancer.

Little do we know what's hovering right under our very noses.

I'm very agitated right now, and know I should get out of this room, take a walk, maybe get some fresh mountain air. I hear sirens in the background as the day becomes steamy. The whining sends chills down my spine. I wonder if I'm coming down with something. It's almost ninety-six outside and I'm experiencing a cold sweat. I should go get a thermometer.

Remember that movie *Phenomenon*, with John Travolta, where this guy starts to become really smart and doesn't know why until he's diagnosed with a brain tumor. And the growth had been applying pressure to the area of genius. I've always wondered, since scientists and researchers know about this area, why hasn't it been activated in us?

And why, in the first place, is *it* deactivated?

I tell you, I truly think the rulers of the world have us by the short hairs.

So, Susie-oh, I bet you don't like being called that, do you? You don't seem like the kind of woman who grew up being called Susie. A lot of people call me John because they think that's my real name, but it's not. *Jack* is my birth name, plain and simple.

My gosh, will that dog ever shut the frack up! It's been barking for over an hour now. You would think the owners would do something about the annoyance. Some people are oblivious. More and more it seems like these days.

I have the news on. I know this is a long letter, but I'm feeling a little lonely right now. Anyway, the story they're reporting is about these scientists who have developed a hormone to increase a child's growth by a couple of inches. The catch is, if they get the injection, they have to take the drug for the rest of their lives.

Leave Nature alone!

I mean, come on!

How far will these researchers take it?

Are human beings becoming nothing more than mutant Earthlings?

Maybe...now that they have a pill for nearly everything. Heaven only knows what people have growing inside of them. It scares me to think about it.

You know, the more I analyze society, the more I begin to understand why you're thinking about suicide. Hell, it makes me want to kill myself. Not that I ever would, because I know I can and am helping people. Maybe that's something you might want to get into. A field where you can be of use to others.

Think about it.

Where are you, Susan?

I'm growing discouraged over my failed attempts to see you. Maybe I should just pack it in and head back to Detroit. Decompress, and then get back to my life, because you know, even though it's not an elaborate existence, it's mine, and I like it.

Maybe that's your problem, you don't like yourself. Is that it, Susan? Is that why you want to buy the farm? Well, if it is, then you're pathetic.

Wait a minute, I just had a thought. What if you're not home? What if you're on a vacation and I don't know about it? After all, I really wasn't definite about coming here. So, maybe all these letters are piling up. When you return you'll find them and think I'm becoming obsessed with you. But no fear, I'm not. Just one of my techniques-persistence.

I'm sorry, Susan, I didn't mean it when I called you pathetic. It's just the frustration talking.

I smell Dad's after dinner odors. He'd disappear into the bathroom immediately after he ate, where he'd smoke a cigarette while taking a crap, and then spray the *Glade* evergreen aerosol air freshener before he came out. A cloud of the three noxious gases would follow in his wake. This was a kind of ritual. The thought of it brings me home.

Did you hear about the couple who had a litter of kids? I think it was seven or eight. I mean, come on, this fertility experiment is going a little too far, don't you think? I wonder how messed up they're gonna be when they get older. And what kind of children they'll produce.

To each their own, I suppose.

There's a lot to be said for the word, *artificial*!

Anywho, I'm not going to delve into this subject right now, maybe later.

The sun sets across the horizon, blazing crimson and violet. Streaks of mercury light pierce through black clouds hovering above me.

The dog has finally shut the hell up.

I wonder if I'll ever sleep again?

Sorry about the long letter.

Talk to you soon!

Your Friend,
Jack Monroe

Dear Susan,

It rained today. Waking me with wet whispers from a long lost guest. I didn't close my window last night. The moisture is a welcome relief, though. I can feel the softness of the humidity coat my skin like a natural lotion. I think of Michigan. I think of you.

The caked mucus loosens from the walls of my nostrils as I blow out dried, lime green boogers. Is that gross or what? I'm sorry. Sometimes, as you know, I can go off on a tangent. But it feels so good to be able to breathe freely once again.

I tell you, this dry air can kill a man!

The weather fits right in today. I'm feeling a little melancholy, while at the same time, nostalgic. I wish I had your phone number so I could call you. Maybe the sound of your voice will make me feel better.

I hear thunder rolling through the skies, like boulders rumbling down a hill. Rain's close. Bet if I stuck my hand out the window and reached into the clouds, I could touch the pulse of the storm! After a while, though, the squall fades into the distance, grumbling like an old man served cold coffee.

Quiet returns to the morning. The only sound is the faint drizzle of rain darkening the earth outside my window. Once in a while I hear someone shuffling down the hall, muffled footsteps on the carpeted planks. It doesn't bother me, though. In a way it's a comfort to know I'm not alone, even though I feel like I am.

Do you ever hear voices, Susan?

I do!

You know, somewhere in time I once read our government can put vibrations, or waves into the air, causing some people to hear voices. You see, they mess with us so much it's not even funny. Could be why I sometimes hear those conversations in my head. I can't decipher any sense from the jumbled noise, nor would I want to.

Bastards!

I know you probably think I'm a mad man. In a way, I am. But, then, aren't we all? Come on, think about it. You must be crazy or insane if you want to kill yourself, right? The person who yells all the time, don't you think they're a little off their rocker. I guess when you live in an insane asylum you're bound to be surrounded by crazies!

Am I right or what?

I can't believe what I just shared with you. I've never told anyone about the voices. I pray you keep it a secret for as long as I have. They're not bad, really. Quite helpful at times. But I don't want to talk about this subject anymore.

The rain has stopped. I re-open my window and wet scents fill the room. I feel young again, as droplets fall onto the dampened cement sidewalks. Cars swoosh by, splashing through swollen pot-holes. I hear the cry of a tourist as the dirt filled water sprinkles his face.

The sun streaks through the dissolving clouds, striking me with laser beam force. I'm energized, filled with a dose of pure vitamin D. *Superman* resurrected!

I think I'm gonna go for a walk, I'm feeling so good. Maybe I'll run into you. I hope so. We could go dancing! Would you like that?

Your Friend,
Jack Monroe

MID-JULY

Dear Susan,

I went to the Shed Restaurant and ordered these wonderful red chili chicken enchiladas. Three rolled corn tortillas stuffed with the most tender chicken I've ever tasted. The dish was smothered in this rich rojo sauce, spicy, yet not over whelming, topped with golden/white cheese. Scrumptious, is all I can say. When the waitress set the plate in front of me, my mouth began to water. You can't get anything like that in Detroit.

Everyone is very kind here at the hotel, at times overly nice. Sometimes I feel like they treat me with kid gloves, as though I were a celebrity or something. A couple of the maids dote on me unnecessarily, but I think it's because they're hoping for a big tip upon my departure.

The skies have been filled with moisture all day, except for a brief streak of sun. It's already dusk and the air smells like fall. The early darkness has triggered the streetlights, and everything's bathed in beige. It feels eerie; I half expect Sherlock Holmes or Jack the Ripper to slink out of the forming mist. The howl of a dog makes me shiver, and I imagine Poe bent crazily over his pale parchment, scratching out *The Tell Tale Heart*.

Golly, I can be so silly at times. Must be the good food making me giddy.

By the way I carry on sometimes, you'd think I was an educated man. Well, I'm kind of half educated, as I like to think. I did get my high school diploma, but only made it through two years of college. I got bored and began to party a lot. Or, I suppose you could say, I started to party a lot and then got bored. How-ever which way you want to look at it, go ahead. It all adds up to the same thing.

Guess I just got tired of memorizing insignificant information.

Plus, who was I kidding? I knew I was bound for the factory.

Not to change the subject too quickly, but I really enjoy reading biographies. Right before I came to Santa Fe, I had just finished reading Anais Nin's diaries'. Wow, what a character!

I believe I made mention of her in an earlier letter.

Anywho!

She was very sexual and didn't hide it. She'd sleep with anyone, poor woman. I think she eventually died of vaginal cancer, but obtained immortality in the meantime.

I don't know why I brought her up again.

Those are the kinds of books I enjoy reading. I don't know why, maybe because I like knowing about people, learning how their personalities and actions changed the course of time. Because, hey, if your biography is in the library, you must've done something, good or evil, to get there.

Maybe I should write your biography: *The Tales of Susan Jordan*, by *Jack Monroe*. First you'd have to tell me a little more about yourself!

I've got to stop watching the news, it just depresses me. Do you think that's one of their intentions, not to inform, but to keep people down? There's so much more going on in the world besides war, murder, and the president.

So, there was a story on one of those news programs like 60 Minutes or 20/20, I can't recall which one. Anyway, they were investigating this popular video game called, *Grand Theft Auto*. I guess the game is about picking up prostitutes, making drug deals, and how to commit a felony. Good times! Anywho, the reporter was saying how bad kid's video games have gotten, and believes a part of the reason why children act the way they do, is because they're allowed to amuse themselves with this pastime.

Dah! Any idiot knows children adapt to their surroundings, and act upon them accordingly.

Each and every day, as I read the papers and watch the news, I begin to understand why you are thinking like you are. I'm beginning to feel the same. The world doesn't seem right. Nothing's getting any better, and there's no one out there who is able to take on the challenge.

I don't mean to sound so glum. Guess it's the weather. You can always blame it on the weather.

Or lack of sleep. Sometimes, Susan, I awake in the middle of the night, shivering in a cold sweat, the sheets and pillow cases soaked. I roll back and forth, falling between drowsiness and awareness. My body swollen red. I'd reach for a glass of water, but I've already drunk it all.

Reluctantly, I rise and go to the sink, turning on the tiny night light. I look in the mirror, and stick my tongue out. A black, fuzzy carpet covers its surface. I quickly rinse my mouth with warm tap water, brushing away the fur.

Susan, I feel I know you well enough now to tell you a real secret. You see, there was a time when I was going to kill myself. Life really sucked and I'd decided to leap off the Ambassador Bridge. Anyway, I won't go into detail of what got me to that point right now, but I was on the vinculum (new word), driving toward Canada, and I was going to stop, get out and jump into the polluted Detroit River below, but something kept me from going through with it.

It was then I began to believe in Divine intervention, and still do to this day. I know there's something out there watching over me, and it makes my life easier. Maybe you should try and think along those lines, see how it goes.

So, instead of plunging to my death, I drove to Windsor and got a hot dog and a cold beer.

I'm tired. I think I'm going to call it a day, even though the sun is just setting and it's only nine o'clock. Good night, Susan. Sweet dreams!

Your Friend,
Jack Monroe

Dear Susan,

The hour is late. A siren snaps me awake. Sweat chills my body. I'm on fire!

I dash to the window but am unable to open the pane. I peer through the dark glass.

The screeches increase as I press my pale-white face against the cool frame, my hot breath blowing small blue clouds on my reflection. They evaporate within seconds. I see no flashing, seizure-causing lights. Everything is opaque from the dim street lamps.

Oh, my gosh, it's not a siren at all, but a damn car alarm. How insensitive! I hate car alarms, cell phones—just about every little device invented over the past three decades. The world is getting scary to me, Susan.

Now I'll be up all night, that's why I sit here writing. You are the only comfort I feel when the world seems bleak.

I picture the living room in my house, which used to belong to Dad, and before that, his dad. The stained beige couch pushed up against the same lemon yellow wall my whole life, and to this day that's where my sofa sits.

I see Mother lying on the davenport in the living room, depressed and crying. "*Jackie!*" she'd call out, and I'd rush to her side. Patting me on the cheek, her hands always cold and clammy, she'd ask. "Jackie, sweetie, get your momma a soda, will ya? And that brown bottle there on the kitchen shelf, would you get that, too? Don't drop it. Thanks, honey."

A few hours later she'd be passed out and I'd sit there all night watching her, listening to her boozed-soaked snoring, afraid the next snort might be her last. Now, when I think of it, what I witnessed was pure unhappiness. Even I couldn't bring a light to her life.

At times I thought she hated me, being so cold and unaffectionate like she was. And in a way, I'm sure she did. But I finally came to terms with the fact it wasn't my fault. Mom was sick, and no one took the time to try and help her.

Like I said earlier, Mom's the driving force in this quest of mine.

I can never explain how much I still miss her to this day.

Do you know what I've always wondered? Who gave names to everything? Like why is a tree a tree, or an ant an ant? Ya know? That's always been a puzzle to me, because if a tree hadn't been named a tree what would it be? Was old Shakespeare right?

A rose by any other name would still smell as sweet.

The unanswerable question?

My body is tired, my mind races around like tiny men on a Merry-Go-Round. I need sleep, but the demon evades me. I see fringes of pink on the horizon as tremors ripple through me, scared to face another day alone.

Maybe I should head home, give up. Is that what you want, Susan?

I need to go.

Your Friend,
Jack Monroe

Dear Susan,

Traffic buzzes in my ears. It's as though I'm standing in the middle of a four lane highway. Well, maybe I'm exaggerating a little bit, but not by much. This is what I get for staying in the cheapest room in the hotel. I paid for another two weeks, and now I'm beginning to wonder if maybe I should go somewhere else.

I've been noticing in the paper these ads for vacation rentals. Maybe I'll look into that over the next couple of weeks. Make it more like a semi-permanent thing. Then we can really get down to work. What do you think, Susan?

I haven't slept at all, and I can feel tiny bubbles popping in my head. I know the tell-tale signs. Within a half hour I'll have a splitting headache; then it'll progress into a migraine. What I need to do is get dressed and go for a walk, get some fresh air, some oxygen to my brain cells, try to stop the invading pain.

I look at my hands, all rough and cracked, tiny slits open through the callused skin, gorges in a dry desert.

A working man's hands.

Your Friend,
Jack Monroe

Dear Susan,

I'm back. I ran as fast as I could, after seeing *that* woman again. Remember, the one who thought she knew me? I spied her coming down the street, so I ducked into a store and tried to hide in the shadows. She walked right by. At first I thought she saw me in the window. Our eyes met briefly, no recognition at all. It was as if she was looking right through me.

Am I crazy or what? I think the next time I see her I'm going to ask who she is, and how does she know me. I should have approached her today. It occurred to me she might be a messenger from you, or maybe knows where you are.

Damn-it!

Why didn't I think of that? Sometimes I need to pay more attention. I'll just keep an eye out for her, maybe go searching for this woman myself. Make an adventure out of it.

I'm beginning to feel sad, and with this sadness comes the bleeding of bad emotions. Sometimes I can control it, turn the tap off before things start flowing, but I don't feel that way in this case.

You know, I want to tell you something. Don't get me wrong, but I believe a lot of people who attempt suicide do it for the attention factor, or they're just feeling really bad at a certain period in their lives. In their mind's eye they have no real intention of killing themselves, they just need help. You're not included in this category, Susan. I believe you contacted me because you are very serious about your intent, and it scares me.

With my other clients, all I had to do was say the right thing, make them feel better about themselves, and they inevitably reconsidered their decision.

Take for instance, this woman I'll call Adele!

Poor girl!

What do you say to a newly widowed 96-year-old who just lost her husband of 75 years?

As the saying goes, time heals all wounds. But then I thought: She doesn't have much time left. Why bother? In spite of that probable truth, I made a convincing argument that her remaining existence here on earth should be filled with love and happiness for her family, friends, and of course, nature!

She got my point.

Adele died nine months later, but at least it was natural, and now she's happy being with Hank, wherever they might be.

You see, Susan, I believe the way you leave *this* dimension has a lot to do with how you end up in the next.

I once knew this woman, "Tammy", who lived with her mother. She was my age. Well, anyway, one Christmas morning she comes home from being out all night, goes to her room and, without saying anything to her mom, blows her head off.

See, now that's someone who's intent on killing themselves. Make no mistakes.

Nobody knows why she did it. Some speculated, broken heart. So in a way, it's a mystery. People will always wonder if they had a part in it. For some, it will eat at them for the rest of their lives. That's what I believe is the worst thing about killing yourself. How it leaves people feeling. That's why suicide letters are so important, and that's why I'm doing what I'm doing. Make sense?

Have you ever had your heart broken, Susan? I'm sure you have. Who hasn't? And those who say they haven't are liars. Everyone's a liar to some degree. Even if it's a small fib, it's still a lie.

Are you lying to me, Susan? Did you lie when you told me you needed my help?

I think to show me your sincerity, let's meet this Thursday, high noon, at the Cross of the Martyrs. How does that sound?

Then I'll know you need me, and I won't feel like I'm wasting my time anymore.

See you then!

Your Friend,
Jack Monroe

Dear Susan,

Where were you? I waited for three hours, standing in the scorching hot sun. You lied to me. How can I ever believe you again? I think I have to end this arrangement with you.

Please don't contact me!

Your Friend,
Jack Monroe

Dear Susan,

Oh, my gosh, I'm so sorry. I didn't mean what I said. We *can* continue with our agreement as long as I know you're reading my letters. That's all that matters, right?

I don't know what got into me. I was so angry, it was as though I'd let my demons out. They controlled my thoughts and actions, leading me down a deep, dark path of loathing and self-hatred.

We've all been there.

It's early morning, and I just ate breakfast. I was starving. Feels like I haven't eaten in a few days. I know I must've, at least I think I have. Everything is beginning to run together, and at times I'm not sure if I've done something, or if it was just a thought with no basis in the real world.

My stay at the hotel is up at the end of the week, and I need to decide what I'm going to do. I have a lead on a rental by the capital, only a ten-minute walk to downtown. I'm not sure though, the owner seemed kind of weird. We've only communicated through E-mail. I had to go to the library to use a computer.

I asked for a week to week rental, and I'm not sure if she's in agreement.

We'll see!

Maybe later I'll take a walk and check the place out. Do you want to come with?

You know, Susan, seriously, maybe you should see a doctor. I've mentioned this before. You could be physically sick. You ever think of that? All these heavy, dismal thoughts could be caused by a few cells out of whack. Bipolar-infested cells. Lacking—what do you call it—lithium?

I'm sure you're not alone either. Probably a lot of people out there who are sick just like you and don't know why. Their lives are seemingly okay, but they don't feel the lightness of being we are supposed to be feeling, if everything's in balance. I believe everyone at least once in their lives, if not fleeting, has thoughts about killing themselves.

Don't you think?

In a way, suicide is premeditated murder.

I sometimes believe our lives are *premeditated*, planned out from the beginning. Yet we can't remember any of the details. How funny is that? It's like someone or something is messing with us-playing around with our lives like we're part of a game.

And what about coincidences? They say there aren't any. Then why, pray tell, is it in the dictionary? Why does it have a definition: the occurrence of events that happen at the same time by accident but seem to have some connection. I don't get it. I certainly have experienced many coincidences in my life.

And you?

Did you know that even though dragon flies have six legs, they can fly, and that the Hawaiian alphabet only has twelve letters? I've discovered these little tid-bits of information off the bottle caps of the Snapple I've been drinking. I love the stuff. I guess it's a new promotion or something.

A person can never learn too much!

My room is heating up again. Facing west, I get the direct late afternoon sunlight beating through my window. I go to the balcony and look down at the plaza. People are milling around like lost ants. The meaty scent of grilled fajitas tantalize my taste buds, making my mouth water. Hey, there's nothing like the smell of charred carne.

The air becomes graveyard still. I once had a friend eat an apple from a tree in a cemetery. I found it rather disturbing. Why, I'm not quite sure. Still, there it is.

Are you alone, Susan?

I am, and find myself being quite content. It seems odd how society deems single people as weird. Like there's something wrong with us. Well, there's not. We're the smart ones, not settling for an unhappy life because everyone else is.

Nope, not me!

Did you know the queen bee can lay 800 to 1500 eggs per day? Now, *there's* a busy bee for you!

Later!

Your Friend,
Jack Monroe

Dear Susan,

I'm sitting in this straight, white metal, upright chair, kind of institutional looking. I like it because it's cold. When I sit in the seat, I get chills. How cool is that? Anyway, the small piece of furniture doesn't really go with the decor of the room, but I like it.

You know, lately when I wake up, which isn't too often, because I seldom sleep, I think to myself how glad I am to be alive. To be able to see the beauty of the earth, to watch nature unfold in front of us. Like seeing a *red headed finch* sitting on a fence, singing out a melody as you walk by. How neat is that?

I wonder if they think we sound like song?

Did you know that termites eat through wood two times faster if listening to rock and roll?

I'm getting antsy. The early evening air is cooling off, still hot, though. If I were home, I'd be strolling around the neighborhood on such a sweaty summer night, listening to the oaks and maples sway softly in the breezes as I make my way around the block I've circled thousands of times. Waving to people I've known for years. Their aging faces lit by moth speckled buzzing lights. With one hand they swat at mosquitoes, while the other holds a warming can of Pabst Blue Ribbon beer, or PBR, as we in Detroit like to call it.

They always offer me one, but I decline, patting my belly and saying, "Sorry, but I just ate and I couldn't put another thing in my stomach."

We all chuckle, and I continue on my way. But I'm sure they whisper to themselves, "Who could refuse a Blue Ribbon, especially on a sweltering hot night like this?"

Do you believe in aliens, Susan?

I do!

Lately more and more, too. I don't know why, but there's something odd about our world right now. Something's changed, like a strange energy has infested humans, animals, plants, and suddenly we're not who we used to be. Even worse, we can't figure out what we're supposed to be. We're slaves. We all work, most of us at jobs we can't stand, and then think it a great success to get a couple of weeks off a year, just to retreat to a vacation you really can't afford to go on anyway.

Then it's back to the grind!

Day in!

Day out!

Day in!

Day out!

Man, no wonder people get depressed.

There I go, flying off into a twizzle again! That's going to be my new favorite word.

Twizzle!

Did you know the average raindrop falls at seven miles per hour? Or that cats can hear ultrasound?

The street lights have come on. They juggle back memories of playing touch football with the neighborhood boys in front of my house when I was a child. The smell of wet leaves and autumn's chilling air. Darkness falling upon us. Shivering in the new cold, trying not to show any weakness, as the copper streetlight casts stretched-out shadows on the tar-cracked cement.

Good times!

Anywho!

Talk to you later; I'm beginning to feel blue.

Your Friend,
Jack Monroe

Dear Susan,

It's the same night as the last letter I wrote you. I can't sleep, and am tired of watching TV. The sky is dark and the stars are out. I saw a slight sliver of the moon earlier as it slipped out from behind a blue-gray cloud, and then disappeared again.

My mood is better; I don't feel as morose. Isn't it weird how that happens? It's like suddenly someone puts a black cloak around you, and you're helpless. But this one wasn't so bad.

I hear the quiet of the night. The occasional lone walker clicking his heels against the empty sidewalk. Echoes from the day bounce off the adobe walls. I get a sense of Christmas. All those joyful times sitting around the tree, holding my breath as Mom opens her gift. Praying she was going to love the dollar scarf I bought for her at Park Pharmacy. Scouring the aisle for what seemed like hours, until I found just the right one.

Mom loved it, as she did all my presents, the few there were.

The little carnival men are starting to run around in my head again. That's what I call them. That's the only way to explain the feeling.

Sometimes when I try to go to sleep, they'll start racing, dulling me into a strange unconsciousness. They haven't been around as much lately, but now they're back.

In force!

Scurrying around like caged cats.

Your Friend,
Jack Monroe

Dear Susan,

I received the note you taped to my door when I returned from my outing. I must have just missed you. Your scent still lingered in the hallway. My heart leapt out of my chest when I saw your handwriting. We have the same style: Parochial school penmanship. It's amazing how many of us write alike. I'll never recover from the Catholic schooling I received, although I am thankful for the nuns who molded me into a principled, moral man.

Thank you very much for the tip on the apartment rental. I contacted the number you gave me, and as you indicated, the directions were on the message machine. I never thought it would be so easy to find a place to rent. I move in this weekend.

Santa Fe's *Great*!

It sounds like you're doing fine, and I understand you've been very busy lately, and that's why you haven't contacted me. Just let me know when you have time! I'm so excited to know you still haven't crossed the final bridge or strung that noose, yet.

Hopefully the urge to do so will dissolve.

We might have crossed paths on your way out and didn't know it. I hadn't been gone for more than a half hour. I suppose it just wasn't meant to be.

Oh well! I'm not going to let the *could-haves* interfere with the *what did's*.

You know what I mean?

I'm *elated* just the same!

Maybe this is a sign our unusual therapy is working. See,

it just takes time to iron out all of the wrinkles, flatten the shirt out, stiff and formal. I love ironed clothes. The clean, pressed feeling against my skin. The scent of laundry soap. I melt when I slip the still-steamy-garment on right after I've creased the sleeves.

Nice!

Did you know that in 1885, the fastest bicyclist was clocked at 154 miles per hour?

I used to like bike riding, but haven't gotten back on a bicycle since the accident.

Sometimes, in the middle of the night, flashing memories zip into my consciousness.

My legs felt like cement as I tried to run from beneath the falling lathe machine. As I covered my head with my trembling arms, I heard a bone crunching crack rip through my ears. I crumbled to the damp floor, and barely remember anything else.

As, you know, I now walk with a limp, my tibia shortened as the shin snapped in half. Naturally my injury never healed right.

I'll never work again. My life-long compensation from the company fits my budget very well, and with the little revenue I get from the suicide letter business, I can enjoy the comforts of life as I know them. All in all, my life ain't so bad, except for the aches and pains I deal with daily.

I can live with that, as long as I know I'm around for a reason.

Again, I sense the feeling of Christmas, and I don't know why. The smell of pine from the tree lot down the block.

Old, scratchy songs blaring from cracked speakers. Fire ripping out of rusted steel drum barrels, licking the brows of the daring few hovering close.

Snow falls gently through the sparkling decorations hung loosely from the street lamps. White angels, silver stars, and evergreen triangular trees. I used to walk down John-R late at night. Stoplights capped in heavy snow, frozen in suspension. Red, green, yellow. Or is it red, yellow, green? Or, green, yellow, red?

You know, I could go on like this for hours!

See, just like that, the sensations of Christmas past are gone.

The maids finally came and cleaned up my room. It was beginning to resemble a sty. I feel much better hanging out in a clean space. I won't be here much longer, a couple of days. I'll try to keep it a little neater, since I'm feeling better. Another bout of altitude sickness, I guess. A common occurrence at this elevation, from my understanding.

I went to the rental apartment to deliver the down payment. The key was just where she said it would be. It's a quaint little place. Box shaped adobe, two stories with a little backyard. It's cozy. When I went inside, the place seemed very familiar, like I've been there before, but how could I, I've only been in Santa Fe for a few weeks now, I think.

Anywho!

The bottom line is, I like the flat, and can't wait until I move in on Friday.

Susan, do you sometimes feel like you're someone else?

Like you've been possessed by a being of some sort who's using your body as a host?

If I'm boring you, don't read this.

Writing is my therapy!

I wonder if I'm becoming *dumb-downed* like the rest of the world. I don't feel like I am. I really don't participate in the distractions of society. I own no computer, cell phone, Ipod, microwave—nothing. The only thing I have is cable, and that's because I love to watch TV. Even though I haven't really been watching a whole lot of the tube while I've been here.

Did you know that you blink over ten million times a year?

Let's see, what other fun facts have I memorized from those damn little bottle caps?

How about, *did you know a sneeze travels out of your nose at 100 miles per hour?*

The night grows silent. I think it's time to hit the hay. I know I'll rest easier tonight knowing you're all right. You've really brightened my day, Susan. Thank you!

I'll be talking to you soon, *Mon Cherie*!

Your Friend,
Jack Monroe

Dear Susan,

Did I ever tell you about Jeffrey? (Guess I don't need to keep telling you that Jeffrey's not his real name. Kind of a professional obligation to protect my client's privacy.) He was this 15-year-old boy who had planned on committing suicide. Thought I lost him once. He had the world going for him: cute, smart, athletic. His demons controlled him, though. Wouldn't let go for the life of him. If you'll pardon the pun. They taunted every dark crease of his depressed, adolescent mind.

He finally came around, though, I don't know why. Maybe he met a girl or something. All I received from him was the return response I include with all my letters, asking my clients to please let me know of their decisions. His "x" was in the changed-your-mind box.

And that's the last I heard from him.

Today I saw a boy who reminded me of Jeffrey, cruising down the street on his ten speed bike, wind whipping through his sun bleached hair, soft brown moccasins tied tight around his ankles; young sweat dripping from his chin, dare, blazing in his eyes. I saw "Jeffrey" today; I thought I lost him once!

Your Friend,
Jack Monroe

Dear Susan,

I know, I know, it's all in my head. Believing because you left me a note that the channels of communication would be re-opened, and I'd be hearing from you again, soon.

There's been nothing.

My mood turns blue! Slate blue, really a cross between this Santa Fe turquoise sky and the intense blue of lapis.

Why?

I thought about trying *not* to contact you, but it's too hard. I'm like addicted to writing these letters. I told myself not to bother again until I received word from you. That's why it's been so long since I've written. I hope you don't think I'm mad. Well, okay, in a way I am. That's a given.

I don't know what to think.

I'm feeling a little crazy.

Maybe I need a break from this.

Roses are red, Violets are blue, I wonder how much longer it'll be, before I see you.

Maybe I'll just lie in bed all day. Watch a little TV. Try to get some shuteye. Nothing wrong with that, is there? I've been working hard, harder than anyone really knows.

Did you know the average speed of a house fly is four and a half miles per hour.

Sometimes I ask myself: What am I doing? Following you across the country like this. Who do I think I am? I'm just a sub-normal, middle-aged man, who has reached his mid-life crisis. That's probably all this is. A way for me to find some salvation, some purpose for my existence.

Do you ever feel that way, Susan? You know, like,

what's the use?

In the past, men didn't have to worry about their mid-life crises because most died before they reached fifty. Did they reach their peak of discontentment at twenty-five?

Poor bastards!

I'm starting to feel better. I believe writing to you takes a lot of weight off my mind. Sorry for sounding angry earlier. Sometimes my frustration over-loads, and all I want to do is scream, lash out, pound my fist against this bland, eggshell wall.

What a yolk!

Susan, do you think when we die, we finally see our purpose and at that moment, our true worth is revealed to us, and we either have accomplished it or not? I wonder what kind of feeling it would be, dying, and then being told we never succeeded with what we were supposed to accomplish.

Bummer!

I believe even if you touch one person in a positive, helpful way, you're a success.

The sunset is marvelous tonight. Burnt sienna, with wisteria streaked skies, cast in a pale peach background, with streaming strawberry clouds dazzling the dusk, like Fourth of July fireworks.

It looks like heaven, and then the stunning beauty changes. Everything turns a white shade of gray. And in an instant, the moment is gone. Whenever I forget about the essence of time, I think of the ticking clock of nature.

Your Friend,
Jack Monroe

Dear Susan,

I feel like I'm losing weight. My pants are looser around my waist, and my underwear isn't as tight. I very well could be dropping a couple of pounds. I really haven't been eating well. I don't know what's wrong.

For the most part, sleep still evades me, and I'm beginning to believe maybe the lack of oxygen in the air is to blame for my restless woes. Thoughts of the swimming pool incident still ripple through me, shivering my soul. You know, the one I told you about, the little girl drowning?

Now, I'm not so sure if it was a dream or not, and I don't want to ask anyone because they might think I'm nuts. I never saw anything in the papers, and there hasn't been a word or notice posted anywhere here in the hotel.

Have I made the whole thing up?

Am I so engrossed with death that I'm imagining a little girl dying?

Or is it you?

Is that how I see you, as a child?

A helpless, vulnerable, lass, whom I can't save?

I'm beginning to feel lost, Susan.

What's going on?

Do you want my help, or not?

Did you know that a ball of glass will bounce higher than a ball of rubber?

Wow, I'd like to see *that*!

I'm hot! It's not even eight in the morning, and already I can feel my sweat soaking the cotton t-shirt I'm wearing. Are you roasting, too? Is it always like this in the summer, or is this year exceptionally steamy?

Susan, let me ask you a question. What would you do if you knew the secrets of the world?

You know, the why's and when's. The who, what, where and how's. Unlocking the mysteries of the universe.

I'd freak!

Not that my curiosity isn't peaked when it comes to finding out what really has happened to us. But right now, for me, I think it would be too much. I'd probably get pissed off. Might even do something harmful to my existence. Ya you know what I mean?

Nope, I'm quite happy right where I am, at this moment, knowing nothing…

Call me lazy, an ignoramus, every name in the book for a coward, I don't care. I'm sure things will reveal themselves soon enough, and that's fine with me.

Then we'll all be enlightened!

What are you talking about, you ask?

Well, think about it, Susan. Isn't there all this talk about veils lifting and the truth coming out? Life changing as we know it? Talk, talk, talk. Everyone watch out for 2012, just like we had to watch out for 1999 when all the computer systems were supposed to fail, and planes would begin falling out of the sky. I think it's well known we don't need faulty systems for aircrafts to crash.

I'm feeling tired, I need a nap.

Your Friend,
Jack Monroe

Dear Susan,

My heart is heavy and my thoughts are clouded with doubt. I feel like I'm stuck inside a toy zeppelin leaking air. I keep running around as the plastic implodes upon itself. My body is molded in rubber; I can't seem to move. I'm dead.

All I see is red!

Tears stream down my face, paving new gullies for upcoming storms. Will I weather this one, can I tie myself tight enough to the mast as the wet winds whip and hammer at me, smashing my tiny boat into sky-scraping swells?

I know I'll drown if I go under; I can't swim.

I need help. Where is the coast guard? The life guards?

Oh, God, please help me. I'll try to keep my head above water as long as I can, but I grow tired. My arms and legs are heavy.

Your Friend,
Jack Monroe

Dear Susan,

I feel so much better today. The headache plaguing me for the past few days is gone. Thank God! I feel like a brand new person. I don't know why it suddenly stopped. Maybe there's something feeding on my brain, and it filled up.

Anyway, all I care about is that I feel so much better than I did.

I wonder what day it is today. I kind of lost track of time during my illness. I can't remember when I'm supposed to be out of this room.

I think today is going to be the break-through day when you come to see me. I can feel your sensations as though you're already here.

But I won't get my hopes up. I learned a long time ago not to have too many expectations, because they never pan out. Especially birthdays. I've never had a good birthday. There was one year, my fortieth, when no one called me. Granted, I don't know many people, maybe a couple, and still, nothing. I was so depressed, I tried to drink my sorrows away and ended up passing out at the Longfellow Elementary School playground. I was so cold when I finally came to, and I felt like I was going to puke. Kids had gathered around me before the morning bell, staring down on my booze filled, bloated body, with questioning, disgust-filled eyes.

I've never been so embarrassed. Staggering home, I wondered how many of the nine million people who share my birthday had a happy one?

But that's neither here nor there. What's important is the

here and now, right?

I guess the only thing to do is be patient. One virtue I've honed down to an art.

Susan, do you know what I think is a shame, and is vandalizing our society? The breakdown of language. I've always maintained that one of the first signs of the potential ruin of a civilization is the destruction of communication. Just look at what the Tower of Babel is all about.

Anyway, here I go again, babbling.

Susan, do you ever wonder if you're just making your life up in your head?

I do!

Surveying my surroundings I wonder just how much of this is real.

I saw *What the Bleep*, six times. I love that movie. My favorite part was when the Shaman was standing on the seashore and noticed some unusual ripples in the water. All of a sudden he sees foreign ships on the horizon, vessels he'd never seen before.

In the movie they theorize that a person doesn't recognize something until they know it exists, and once the image is in your mind, you'll always see it. Hence, the boats the natives had never seen before, were invisible, until the ships were seen by the Shaman and he opened the eyes of the islanders to the invaders.

Not that it did them much good. At least they got to see the faces of their killers.

Anyway, when you think about it, Susan, there could be a lot of things out there we're not seeing. I just wonder if they see us?

I sometimes feel like I live within four white walls. There's nothing stimulating about them. The sheet rock is cut to perfection, no abnormalities. Joints feathered. How boring would it be if we lived in a non-abnormal environment. I guess it would be normal.

Did you know Alaska has the highest percentage of people who walk to work?

Good for them!

I used to walk to work every day. The shop was very close to my house. I loved it.

Talk to you later!

Your Friend,
Jack Monroe

AUGUST

Dear Susan,

I awoke early this morning, and saw angels sitting on my bedpost. Are you among them now, is that why they came to see me? I'm scared. What if you went ahead and did it? You know, killed yourself. I'd have no way of knowing.

Would you do that to me, Susan? Would you throw me into grief without the slightest warning?

I wanted to ask the angels if they've seen you, and why were they here, but they vanished right in front of my eyes, and I never got a chance to inquire.

What should I do, Susan?

I'm going out of my mind with worry. I don't normally believe in signs, but I bet you me, that sure was one.

Do you think I'm crazy?

Well, I am—already confessed. So you can stop asking yourself that question now, okay?

The sky is night-dark. Storm clouds drift in front of the Luna turning it into a melon ball. Thunder rolls above as lightning licks the ground with its hot, bolting tongue.

I sit before my reflection in the black mirror of the window. Flashes electrify me, the beeswax candle flickers from my heavy breath. I feel an anxiety attack coming on. I try to calm myself with soft humming.

It helps a little.

Truth is, I'm terrified!

Each and every day that goes by my heart becomes older, tougher, like sun dried rawhide. I'm at my wits end. I don't know what to do anymore. I know the smartest thing would be to pack it up and head out. Shake the dust from my feet. I know how this is going to end, and I know I'm going to get hurt.

Please, Susan, don't hurt me!

Your Friend,
Jack Monroe

Dear Susan,

You won't believe what happened to me the other night. I was sitting here just about ready to write you a letter when this heat wave blasted through me. I felt clammy. My mouth became dry and salty. Then all of a sudden, I'm rushing to the bathroom, heaving into the porcelain bowl. I have no idea what brought it on, but the rest of the night, I couldn't get out of bed. For some time, I lay there shivering, then hot...shivering, then hot.

Maybe it was something I ate!

I feel much better today, though! The cramps are gone, and I'm able to keep down a little food, mostly saltine crackers and water. All I want to do is sleep, then maybe this nagging headache will go away.

Outside my window shines a periwinkle sky. I can see the mountains in the distance, as a faint hint of smoke rises over the tree line. Must be a fire somewhere in the forest.

Did you know slugs have four noses?

Talk about being nosey!

Your Friend,
Jack Monroe

Dear Susan,
Have you forgotten about me?

Your Friend,
Jack Monroe

Dear Susan,

I went for a stroll last night, after the air cooled. The city was convent quiet, just the hum of the tungsten-lit street lights. The birds already nestled in their nests, heads tucked beneath feathered wings. I could dig being a bird. Maybe a blue-jay, I love their color. Can you imagine a world without them?

I can't remember the last time I had a real conversation. A verbal one, and not one-sided. I don't really miss it, though, talking to people. I'm not very good verbally, and am a worse listener. I pretend a lot to be paying attention, but then all of a sudden, I'll kind of wake up and realize I have no idea what they're talking about.

It's quite embarrassing!

Did you know the hummingbird weighs less than a penny?

Have you ever been to Minneapolis?

What a beautiful town! When the day is right, and the lakes are glistening, the blue sparkles off the glass towers downtown making the place look like Emerald City from the Wizard of Oz!

A horse of a different color.

A horse is a horse of course of course. Have you ever heard of a talking horse?

Of course. Mr. Ed.

Geeze, it sounds like I'm losing my mind.

I feel sweat dripping down my armpits.

Does the heat ever stop?

The buzzing is back; I await the arrival of the little carnival men. They scare me sometimes, because I don't know where they come from, or where they are going. Maybe I should get a CAT scan, or whatever they call it. See if there's something in my brain that shouldn't be there.

Could be why all my thoughts and words have been so garbled here of late.

What if I have a brain tumor? Would I let them operate, slice my scalp open with a sharp scalpel? It'd be neat if they took Polaroids while they were in there so I could see my brain afterward. I bet you there aren't too many people who can say they saw their own cranium opening like a flower to expose the honeycombed brain underneath.

What if they crack me open and find a peanut sized brain? That was one of Dad's favorite sayings. *He has a peanut brain*. My father had quite a few colorful descriptions for people. Once in a while, I'll catch myself sounding like him. I just shake my head to rid myself of the mannerism.

At least I don't look like him; brawny, and dark. My features are more like my mother's, small boned and orange, yet strong. It's funny, when I was a young boy, Dad always seemed so large, and loud, but then as I became an adult, I realized he was kind of puny and smelled funny. I felt sorry for him. Exactly why, I do not know.

I hope you're still well!

Your Friend,
Jack Monroe

Dear Susan,

There's someone at the door! I crawl over, squatting close to the key hole. I feel like *Alice in Wonderland*—slowly shrinking.... my pale blue party dress hanging on me like a drape.

Another knock!

Hard!

Swift!

"Susan!" the voice nips. "It's Judith, I know you're in there. I watched you go into this room, plus, I heard you moving around."

I hold my breath, freezing my cells, watching through the church-key slit, as the intruder's lime-green linen slacks pace back and forth.

It's the woman from the plaza!

She must have followed me. Knows I am in contact with you. Thinks maybe you might be hiding out here.

I wish!

"Susan, come on, open up! This is ridiculous. No one's seen or heard from you for three weeks, now."

Ah-hah! So, it's not just me. You're not talking to anyone. I guess you did leave the city, went on some sort of vacation. I understand you wanting to be alone. Think things out; contemplate your next move.

Oh, what a relief! I'd begun to believe you'd abandoned me. But all this time you've been on holiday.

I still hear Judith hovering outside my door. My knees knock against each other, creating static sparks. I hope I don't set myself on fire. What a lousy way to go!

"Fine, be that way! If you don't want to see or talk to anyone, there's nothing I can do about it. You know where you can find me."

I listen to her hollow-heeled shoes stomping down the padded hallway like a petulant child. I'm still holding my breath. I hear the stairwell door slam shut, and then the silent echo of emptiness.

I exhale!

Now what?

Your Friend,
Jack Monroe

Dear Susan,

I moved out of the hotel!

After *that* crazy woman, Judith came banging on my door, I gathered my things, and snuck out. I'm all paid up, so they won't really care if I leave a day early. Lucky for me I can go to the rental; there's no one there.

How obtrusive!

I hope she doesn't follow me!

Anywho!

I now sit in the dirt backyard on a weather-worn picnic table, on a patch of grass. A slab-board fence keeps the neighbors from seeing in. For everything being so close to everything, this place is quite quiet and peaceful.

It's kind of funky, all used furniture and decorations, as though she had arrived empty handed and this is what she had collected over the years. Kind of gypsy like. Clean, though. Plus, there's a great music selection; everything I like. Go figure.

I appreciate the tip. Maybe, when you come over you'll have to tell me about the woman who lives here. I find it odd that there are no pictures around, anywhere.

I suppose she's just not into photos.

It's so nice here. The softening summer sun slides behind the fence, cooling the back in a pool of shade. Whirls of weakening winds wisps my chestnut hair; I brush it to the side and hold my palm down on the yellow pad. A spatter of ink smudges my next word, my thumb-print dried in time.

Your Friend,
Jack Monroe

Dear Susan,

Did you know that cats have over one hundred vocal sounds?

Susan, Susan, Susan! Where art thou Susan?

I saw a turtle dove this morning, sitting on an overhead wire. It was beautiful! Its gray-brown feathers shining in the early sunlight, sleek in its profile. It's needle-beaked head bobbing in and out, as it takes flight, flapping noisily out of sight.

Flying dinosaurs.

I've been thinking a lot about death lately, and how final it is. There's no two ways about it: once you're gone, you're gone. There's no turning back, and in a way that scares me. Because what if I was just in a bad mood one day and decided to off myself? Maybe if I had waited another day, things would have been different, don't you agree?

As a boy, I used to pack up salmon and butter sandwiches, (canned salmon on Wonder white bread spread with Parkay margarine. Ick!). Anywho, during the summer, I'd walk down to Green Acres Park and watch the baseball games. I loved it, sitting there as day turned into dusk, casting rusty reflections from the hazy setting sun. Then the lights would go on, as the stands explode triumphantly with another score by the home team. The crowd's cheering and clapping, echoing off the somber faces of their rivals.

I never played sports. I was kind of clumsy!

No loss!

I spent a lot of time alone as a child—no brothers or sisters to play with. No cousins either. The neighborhood kids were always a little standoffish, so there were no close bonds made.

Then as an adult, I'd go out for beers with the guys. We'd usually talk shit. Mostly about getting laid, or the latest football or baseball game. You know that kind of stuff. Once in a while I'd go bowling with them. But I didn't then, as now, consider any of them to be my friend, even after all these years.

So, in a way, I guess I'm friendless.

Golly, isn't that pathetic? Alone and unloved.

Could be why I'm latching on to you this way? Wow! Maybe I need to back off, stop the letters for a while before I scare you away. Guess I am being a little overbearing.

Do you text?

Should I get a cell phone so we can communicate voice to voice? Would it be more convenient for you? I'll have to look into it, if you'd like, although I swore off cell phones because I believe they're unhealthy. Rot the brain kind of thing.

Do you believe the craze, though! People walking around with these devices pressed against their ears. I just don't get it, everyone distracted, and not paying attention to where they're going. How did we ever survive without them?

There I go again, getting all dark and cynical. But come on, don't you think this world is *fracked up*? Sorry, I don't mean to get angry, but when I think about all the craziness, and then ask myself why, when it doesn't have to be like this, I get a little mad. Especially when there's a simple solution.

Just stop!

Stop the wars, stop the destruction, stop the killing!

What's so hard about that?

Guess no one listens any more.

Did you know that the San Francisco Cable Cars are the only mobile National Monument?

Have you ever been to Frisco?

Talk about a beautiful city!

On every corner a scenic view. You can walk down Jones Street and see the bay from the top. Coit Tower, a monument to firefighters, stands gray and erect, against the sea sky. And the smells; I felt like I was in a carnival. It was great!

Anyway, I went to the city by the bay for a little vacation a few years back, okay, more like twenty. My timing wasn't so good, though. I arrived in October of '89, the year of the quake.

Listen to this, I was strolling around the Mission District just doing the usual tourist things, when suddenly I hear a rumbling. I'm moseying by a furniture store thinking to myself they must be moving something pretty heavy. Then all of a sudden, the windows begin blasting out, and the ground beneath my feet starts to roll, almost knocking me to the pavement.

When I recovered my balance, I noticed people were running out of the surrounding buildings, yelling and screaming. Then, it stopped. I was electrified. To experience, such a powerful natural phenomenon, and to walk away from it unscathed, to me, that's a miracle!

You know what I'm talking about?

Right?

Your Friend,
Jack Monroe

Dear Susan,

Oh man, Susan, it poured earlier. I decided I needed some fresh air, so I went outside, and the skies were black and streaked with lightning. The clouds rolled together in thunderous rumbles. Torrential rains immediately pounded down on the dry, dusty yard.

When the first drops hit the dirt ground, I could see miniscule mushroom clouds forming from the impact. The moments were sensational. Thoughts of autumn are creating a sense of sadness, a lingering nostalgia. I want to go home. I miss my house, the air, the pesty dog down the street that barks all the time.

I'm lonely, Susan, and bored with myself. What am I to do?

Fifteen minutes later, the storm passes. Everything is quiet, even the birds haven't made a peep yet. I listen to the echo of water dripping from the eaves, clipping stunned leaves as the liquid pebbles splash to the muddy ground.

Your Friend,
Jack Monroe

Dear Susan,

The March before Mom killed herself; Dad, in an attempt to jolt some life back into our family, took us to Florida to see my mom's parents. I had no recall of what they looked like, just the 2D images from the few scattered frameless pictures lying around.

They argued all the way down. Luckily for me the tips I made as a paper-boy afforded me a Walkman. I kept the blue sponged headphones on the entire trip. I'd never seen the ocean before, and when the green surf rose over the white sandy beaches hugging Hwy. 1, I thought I'd died and gone to heaven.

All I wanted to do was scream at my dad to stop the car, let me out, tell him he can pick me up on the way back. This is my vacation, too, and I should be able to spend it the way I want.

So there!

Once we got to Grandma and Grandpa's house, Mom stopped crying long enough to put her bag in the room she and Dad would be sharing, and then started hitting the booze. There was no way I'd get to the beach now.

My disappointment was deep and vengeful. I had to figure a way out.

I knew in a couple of hours, they'd all be looped enough for me to sneak away, but then the sun would be down, and the sky dark, and I wouldn't be able to see a damn thing, so what would be the point.

Nope, immediate action was called for, a plan, maybe feign illness, go to my room, climb out the window. Sometimes it's so easy, it's ridiculous. I'd be right back, no one would know I was gone, then when I returned I would come out, saying I'm feeling better. I wouldn't be gone long. I just wanted to put my feet in the froth of the sea.

So, that's exactly what I did.

The timing was impeccable, the adults were in deep discussion, and barely even noticed me when I excused myself from the dinner table. Mom was on her second bottle of wine, and Dad was slamming down the high-balls like there was no tomorrow. Good thing no one was driving that night.

Anywho!

I snuck down to the cooling shore, tide still out for the evening. I moved closer to the foamy white water, looking back over my shoulder to make sure I hadn't been made. My gaze turned back to the surf. Soft green, reminding me of a Granny Smith apple, swelled toward me, spraying salt kisses upon my brow. Pirate winds slapped my cheeks, tossing my hair like an un-piloted ship.

I moved closer, caught in some kind of translucent trance.

All of a sudden I feel this seething pain coarse through my foot. As I look down, I see this florescent purple ballooned alien flapping helplessly on the sand. Long spaghetti like tentacles floated in the white wash-blue and violet strings, dangling from the clear mushroom shaped body.

I glanced along the shore. There were hundreds of these creatures stranded on the beach. It was amazing I'd made it so close to the water without being attacked.

Six seconds passed before the scream that had lodged in my throat bellowed out as I fell to the sand, reaching for my swelling toes. The sting was searing as the venom from the Man of War released an allergic reaction that took me three weeks to recover from.

Dad had to get back to work, so my parents returned to Detroit without me. I'd fly home after I began to feel better. I didn't want to go. I wanted to stay in sunny Florida, go hang out on the beach, live a life of quiet and ease, get away from the weight of constant anger.

That didn't happen, though.

My grandparents shipped me home ASAP, seemed like they couldn't wait to get rid of me. See, Susan, I've never been a favorite of anyone's.

I never returned to Florida!

Your Friend,
Jack Monroe

Dear Susan,

I'm very sad today, and I don't know why. I got a good night's sleep. But when I awoke earlier this morning, I felt unhappy, filled with discontent. Even now, I feel like running away, finding some small town where no one knows who I am and drink myself to death.

What is happening to me?

I never used to think like this. When I was younger there seemed to be more hope, more time to fulfill my dreams. Now, though, my life feels desperate, like I have to hurry and get something done, yet I don't know what it is. I feel like I'm losing my faith. Maybe it's just a bad day.

Do you think they have anything to do with it?

Damn-it to hell, I miss my home.

I should go to a movie, get out, do something social, even if it is by myself. I feel like I've been in a fog.

You know, Susan, I had an idea the other day you might be interested in. I'd like to run it by you, see what you think. You've heard me talk about the huge house back in Hazel Park—lots of space and rooms, not far from culture, restaurants. Anyway, I was wondering if maybe after you figure all this stuff out, you might want to come live with me.

I won't charge rent. The house has been paid for since before Dad died. The yard is spacious, if you wanted to till a garden. Oh, and how wonderful it would be to sit in the back on a sultry summer night, smell the greenness of the corn stalks rising to meet the sky.

We can barbeque, anything you want, maybe some fresh vegetables from the vines.

Doesn't that sound good? And in the winter we can keep the fireplace stoked with burning embers.

What do you think?

You can trust me not to be intrusive. Your space is just that, your space, and vice versa. Think about it. You don't have to move in right away, perhaps somewhere down the line. Whatever the case, the offer will remain open.

Did you know that brain waves can be used to run an electric train?

Shhhh, be quiet for a minute, Susan, I think I hear something outside the door.

I'll be right back.

I was wrong!

At first I thought it was *that* damn woman again, Judith what's her name. But how could she have found me? I think this time though I would have opened the door and addressed her face to face, tell her to leave me alone, and that I don't know where you are either.

But it was nothing.

Am I starting to hear things?

Do you think sooner or later everyone goes crazy? The brain just can't take it anymore, and begins to crack.

Has it ever happened to you, Susan?

Do you think you can go crazy if you're insane?

The other day I saw a Navajo woman walking down the street. She couldn't have been more than forty. Thin, frail, with turquoise beaded necklaces dangling from her out stretched hand. A black velvet board splashed with sterling silver earrings is perched on her hip.

Her hair is shiny black, pulled back with a turquoise leather hair ribbon. Uneven cut bangs hang over her forehead. Her face is compact and brown, crinkled from decades of squinting in the sun. She smiles at me with an empty mouth as we pass by each other.

Her name is Carmelita!

I wonder if she ever thinks about ending it all?

Your Friend,
Jack Monroe

Dear Jack,

I hope this stays between us. It's important that we keep this secret silent. What if we die, and don't know it. Just pick up in another life without recalling the last one?

Could our existence just be a constant loop, going round and round and round in the circle game. You know that old song of Joni's? We could be doing the same things over and over, repetitious monotony. Is there any way out?

Do you think good ole' Abe knew his assassin was afoot, and decided to take the bullet head-on.

No pun intended.

Oh, by the way, I'm back. Sorry I haven't contacted you sooner. Don't ask me where I've been, because to be honest, I can't recall anything. It's as though I've misplaced a good chunk of time.

I feel like I'm some kind of centrifuge, colliding, discolliding, turning matter into pulp. I don't feel like I'm *me* anymore, like my whole being has been displaced. What is going on, Jack? I'm scared!

Am I a split atom?

My other self is sharing my consciousness and I don't know who they are. All I know is that they must cease to exist.

And you wonder why I want to kill myself. How long could you last being like this?

I found all of your letters, they were jammed in the mailbox. It took me a while to find the key, but after I did, I labeled it and hung it on a nail.

Anywho, enough with the babble.

Jack, I want to know if I can rely on you to help me find this imposter that has been leading my life, using my body as a host, which I believe is happening. I tell you, if we can figure out this mystery, I might reconsider my intentions.

Will you come over?

I'm at home now, sitting in the yard, back pressed against the heated wooden-planked fence I built by hand. I love my space. It's not much; the Cyprus tree leaves fade into lemon-yellow as the summer sun continues to bleach the foliage. My old, dried out dartboard hangs on the wall, millions of pin-points cover the surface, like the dark galaxy. Maybe I'll toss a few while I wait for your response.

Please, Jack, hurry; I can't take this craziness anymore!

Your Friend,
Susan Jordan

Dear Susan,

I finally found the mail-box key. It was right there in front of my eyes on a small nail, labeled. Am I a nut, or what? I found your letter. How nice of you to write me at last, and now I understand why you haven't been in contact. *That* weird woman Judith was right, you were on vacation. I feel better now.

Anyway, just wanted to drop you a quick note to tell you about the key, and, yes, of course I'll help you find your Doppleganger!

Your Friend,
Jack Monroe

Dear Susan,

The aging wind is like a rolling wave you can hear coming on, but can't see. The trees and leaves rustle, like a fugitive ghost dashing by.

Susan, I ask you, is there no way home?

Will we be forever imprisoned, cast into the depths of hell, Dante's Inferno, death after life. I'm fooling myself and you. I'm no one's knight in shining armor, my shores behold no bright horizons. I bask in a chilled sun; pale white, my skin becomes.

I wish I weren't so fond of you. I truly desire to walk away, not get any deeper involved in this cross-bearing weight you carry. I feel doomed and dark, like a condemned con.

I see you cry in the mornings, and there's nothing I can do, no words to console you. Dormant thoughts provoke you, I feel like I'm losing the battle. How could I possibly be of any help?

Your Friend,
Jack Monroe

Dear Susan,

Did you know that chewing gum while you peel onions will prevent you from crying?

It's early morning, and I'm cold. I think the temperature dropped down to the forties last night. I'd left the window open slightly, so I was freezing when I woke up.

I still have a chill!

The leukemic sun plays peek-a-boo with the clouds, while laser streams of light burst through the outline of the black thunderheads. I'm reminded of the Great Lake's skies—fluffy, creamy bundles of steaming rain, gathering on the bloody horizon.

My favorite Great Lake is Huron! The sandy shore, speckled with huge boulders once covered with the crystal blue water. During the summer, I'd drive up to Lexington— it's right in the thumb of Michigan—and sit on the shore, watching the sun rise. The swallows would soar above me, swooshing up and down, back and forth, like carefully crafted kites.

I feel sick to my stomach this morning. I ate a Mallow Cup yesterday. Heaven only knows how old it was. I found it at Senor Murphy's Chocolate Shop, located at the La Fonda Hotel. A historical landmark right down town. The Inn is well over four hundred years old. Santa Fe's full of old structures. It just goes to show you that mud and straw buildings do hold up over time.

The world scares me, Susan!

Have you ever felt the rush of fear? That breath-catching, cold-sweating, out of control fright?

I have!

One time I drove to Chicago to see the Red Wings play the Black Hawks in a pivotal season-breaking hockey game. I love the *Wings*! Anyway, I decided to stay the night because the game ended really late and I didn't feel like spending five hours driving home.

As I made my way up to my motel room, this guy comes out from no-where, holding a switchblade, and points it at me. He's really close now, maybe six yards away, and I hear him hiss, "*I want you.*"

Quickness has never been my forte, but that night I was faster than lightning. I unlocked the bolt and whipped into my room, shutting the door behind me. The wood slammed in his face. I slipped the chain lock through the slit. Would it hold, I wondered as he started pounding on the barrier.

He kept screaming at me to let him in, said he was going to kill me. I knew he had to be on something, *PCP* maybe. Anyway, I called the front office, and I guess they notified the cops. It didn't take them long to get there, either. Probably had 911 on speed dial. I heard the guy cursing me as he fled the scene.

After an interrogation, the police left, leaving me alone, terrorized to the bone.

The incident confirmed my belief, that yes, I do live in an insane asylum.

I drove home that night and have never returned to the Windy City again.

Plus, the Red Wings lost.

I'm tired, Susan. These waves of sleepiness wash over me

like a high tide. My eyes are blurry, and I can barely read the words I scribble to you.

Did you know the state of Maine has 62 lighthouses?

Do you think someone can have talent, but no creativity?

Or have creativity, but no talent?

I would think they would go hand in hand.

I'm bored!

Tired of my life.

The interminable moments ahead of me!

Does this sound like the summer of my discontent? What a novel novel!

I'm sorry, Susan. I confess it: I'm just being silly.

My mind is fried, thunder rattles through my brain. I need to get a good night's sleep tonight. I can feel my nerves sizzling from lack of rest. I don't know what I'm going to do if I have to stay up all night, again.

You might be hearing from me later!

Your Friend,
Jack Monroe

Dear Jack,

Do you find it strange, both of our mothers dying when we were children? Is that why I suddenly feel such a close bond to you? I finished the rest of the letters piling up in my absence.

To be honest, Jack, I couldn't remember who you were at first. Then, as I read your writings, I recalled having asked you to come to Santa Fe to help me. How could I forget something so important? I was in Detroit at the time, checking on my Dad's house I'd put up for sale after he died six months ago.

That's where we met, right? You mentioned the rendezvous in one of your letters, but my memory draws a blank. I only see disjointed fragments, everything else eludes me.

I believe you though, Jack. You seem like a very honest and sincere man.

Sorry for being such a mystery woman, if I had known you were coming, I wouldn't have left town, or wherever I went. Maybe you're right, Jack. Maybe I should go see a doctor. These blackouts are getting worse, but then they would just dope me up with drugs and I'd never find the true source of my problem.

But with your help, Jack, I think we can solve this dilemma, once and for all.

I sit on my balcony watching the moon rise over the misty foothills. A blue-cheese ball with shaded pock marks, so close I bet if I reached out I could circle my finger around one of the craters.

Jack I don't think it's me who wants to commit suicide, I

think it's my assassin who's infiltrated me, and now lives amongst my thoughts.

I think she wants me dead!

I'm scared!

Your Friend,
Susan Jordan

Dear Susan,

I thought I saw you in the square the other day. Just for a second your profile filled my eyes, and then when the woman turned and I saw her full face, I realized it wasn't you. It made my heart drop a little, you know, the bleeding organ became slightly heavier.

Ultra-violet rays crease through the balcony window, spraying me with pink-smoky-winds blowing in my direction from some huge fire in Los Alamos. The blaze is changing the sun into a burnt mango ball as it recedes into a pale gassy haze. It feels apocalyptic!

Anywho, *the first telephone book published in 1878 only contained fifty names.*

Those days are gone, forever!

Did you ever think you would know a person with so much crap in his head?

Susan, have you ever come across a time where you wished you'd done something different? You know, said *that* other thing, crossed *that* other street, thought *that* other thought. Have you ever added up all your regrets, threw them into a sack, and clobbered yourself over the head with them?

And in the end it all added up to the same thing, nothing but a headache!

Is this all life has to offer?

Thinking you did the wrong thing, and that's why you're here.

Did you know almonds are a part of the peach family?

I can feel the streaks of pain as a migraine approaches. I

want to try and ward it off before it reaches full potential. I'm going to say good-bye for now, Susan. I'll be talking to you soon!

Your Friend,
Jack Monroe

Dear Susan,

You would not believe how bad my brain-splitter got the other night. I thought my head was going to implode. I could feel my heavy heart beating—slowly, pounding out of my chest, quaking my cranium. I cried all night. The Advil didn't help, nor the six bananas I ate. Somewhere I read or heard that the yellow fruit was filled with potassium, and helped to ward off headaches. So much for that bit of folk medicine.

Look, I used two words ending with *ium*—cranium and potassium.

Anyway, I'm feeling much better today.

Sometimes I imagine a life without stress and worry. Existing in a calm and cool atmosphere, enjoying the sunny day, listening to music outside.

Do you like music, Susan?

I truly believe music was sent from the heavens!

This place I'm staying in, is *great*! The woman has almost the identical music collection as I have. Now how weird is that? I've heard the saying, "It's a Santa Fe Thing," but hey, come on. Some of these albums I didn't think anyone else owned.

Strange, yet groovy at the same time.

I can't decide which vinyl is my favorite. I like them all.

The clouds are finally burning off the mountain, and slight ghost images begin to appear behind the spreading mist. The air is cool and moist. Hopefully, I can go for a walk later, stretch my legs, pump hot adrenaline through my heart.

Your Friend,
Jack Monroe

Dear Susan,

I escaped today!

I snuck out to the parking lot pretending I was a secret spy who had been made. I needed to get away before I was caught, and tortured.

Cloaked by the dark, I sneaked through this hole in the fence I'd discovered a few weeks ago. It was covered by a bush. When I first saw the tangled tin, it reminded me of hopping my neighbor's fence as a child, and sitting under Mrs. Penn's grapevines eating handful upon handful of these sweet-sour concord grapes.

She'd see me through her kitchen window, but pretended not to notice the small boy crouched in the shadows of the green ribbon plant. I felt comfortable there, smelling the humid earth. The scents always smells like worms. My favorite time of day was sunset, when the air would cool down and the grass would ignite its perfume.

I slipped through a cracked wall and found myself in a narrow alley. Checking over both shoulders to make sure nobody saw me, I cantered down a dusty path that lay at the passage's edge. I felt free, exhilarated…scared.

Westerly winds snapped the sun's rays against the turquoise credit union sign, flashing an SOS signal to oncoming traffic.

Where was I going?

Fear and tension crept back into my spine, all bravery and courage washed away by the unknown, the unplanned, the unexpected. But, then, nothing was to be expected. I rushed back to the grapevine, telling myself I'll try again another time.

Your Friend,
Jack Monroe

Dear Susan,

Did you know that frogs don't drink? If that's true, then those Budweiser commercials are nothing but false advertising. How do you like them cookies?

If you haven't been able to tell by now, I'm a little spastic today. I just don't feel right, which seems to be the frequent complaint as of late. Oh well, what am I to do?

I see the square steeples of the St. Francis Cathedral in the distance, as the bells chime nine. Must be time for Mass. Maybe I'll go. I haven't been in a church for I don't know how long. Lightning will probably strike me as I go in.

Wouldn't that be funny?

I know you think I'm stalling, evading the inevitable, unanswerable question, if I'll help you assassinate your assassin. I'm not sure if I can, Susan. That's not my field of work. I'm a scribe, not a mercenary. You have to understand. My thoughts, and prayers are with you, and hell, for that matter, so am I, but when it comes to this, I wouldn't even know where to begin. Plus, you know the best way to get away with something is if you do it alone, because then no one else knows you're the culprit.

I won't blame you if you're mad at me, because really, who do I think I am?

Barging in on your life like this, pretending I'm Sir Lancelot or something. Your champion until death do us part. And then, when you really need me, I blow you off. What kind of friend is that, I ask myself? You must think I'm a buffoon. Which I am! I've proven that to myself time and again.

A tear streams down my face, and my heart feels heavy.

Your Friend,
Jack Monroe

Dear Jack,

I'm so depressed today. I had another black-out, can't remember anything. I don't know what to do. If I go to a doctor they'll surely lock me away. Then it'd be too late; I'd never be able to kill myself.

Tiredness cloaks me. I drag my gravity bound body across darkened universes, captured, imprisoned in a world I do not belong to, nor it, to me. There is no reason to stay here any longer.

I am not afraid of the alternative, hell, it's all dimensional anyway, don't you think, Jack? We just take a step to our left or right, and everything's different, except you're the same.

I hope not. That's what I'm trying to get away from.

Now that's irony!

When I arose earlier, I was in my bed and my clothes were different. I have no sense of time, so I'm not sure how long I was gone. I stare out over the falling Jemez mountains. Shades of apricot dot the tree line. The satin sun stimulating my skin with its radiant light.

It scares me not knowing where I've been, or what I've done. Maybe I should install a camera downstairs by the front door, to keep track of my comings and goings. Could be there's a pattern forming that I can dismantle.

My mind is calming down after writing you. How comforting it is to have someone out there whom I can relate to. Maybe some time this week you can come over, we can toss a game of darts, have a beer or two.

Let me know what's good for you!

Your Friend,
Susan Jordan

Dear Susan,

Did you know the sitcom Friends *was at first going to be called* The Insomnia Café?

Can you tell I've been drinking a lot of Snapple lately? As a result my fun facts are increasing. So is my waistline!

I've been feeling a little better for the most part. I don't know what causes the black cloud to hover over me. Two flies are caught between the screen and the open window. They buzz around frantically trying to figure a way out, when all they have to do is go the way they came.

Maybe they're ADD products.

Who knows?

Who cares?

I feel like I'm flushing thoughts out of my brain with these letters to you. Since I've been writing, my whole being seems lighter, almost ethereal. It's as though I'm getting to know myself through you.

How is that possible?

Sometimes I can hear myself in you, and you in myself.

How is that possible?

Is it kind of like a Yin/Yang thing. We're the same, but not. I wonder what it would be like if things were the opposite, I am you and you are I. Yang/Yin.

Hey, listen to this poem I wrote while I was sitting out back.

Patty Melt
Throw me on a grill and let me sizzle,
Outside slight signs of haze and drizzle.
Bikes lined up evenly in three,
Leaves above me empty of the Cyprus tree.

Flip me just once and let me simmer,
As August days turn from bright to dimmer.
Birds chirp above me in quiet dusk like songs,
As distant church bells strike six vibrant gongs.

Cheese me with Cheddar, Jack or the tangy Swiss Miss,
Touching my lips like a soft delicate kiss.
You melt and coat the four corners of my world,
My earth went spinning, whipping in a whirl.

Slide me on dark bread with caramelized onion,
As I watch the fading summer sun descend.
The doubts and fears of the day I felt,
Have all disappeared as I eat my Patty Melt.

Throw me on a grill and let me sizzle.
Outside slight signs of haze and drizzle.
Bikes lined up evenly in three,
Leaves above me empty on the Cyprus tree.

Wow! What do you think?

Granted, I'm no Emily Dickinson, but, hey, at least I'm willing to try.

You're probably great, Susan. I wish you would let me read some of your work. I like poetry, if I can understand the piece. Like this one I'll always recall, but can't remember the poet's name. *encouraged by boredom, eve went in search of an apple, she was tired of bananas.*

I think that's hilarious!

I know no others.

Your Friend,
Jack Monroe

Dear Susan,

Last night, out of shear boredom I strolled down San Francisco Street and found myself across from the Lensic Theater. There was a long line of people curving around Burro Alley. Some lazily leaned against the bronze donkey lugging a bag of sticks. I slipped between a man and a woman, and walked down the quiet side street, discovering a fancy French restaurant tucked away. White lights dangled from the pale façade, as I noticed the café was empty; probably had their rush already.

A vapor of garlic floated through the air, as I listened to mumbled chatter from the remaining tables. Tinny French violin music squeaked out of the small speakers angled in the corners, tickling me ears. I felt the urge to dance, shout out to everyone.

"My name is Jack Monroe, and I'm glad to be alive."

Being the shy man I am, I kept quiet.

I felt free!

I felt invisible!

A woman, sitting against the wall, thought she saw me, her eye catching mine. Her stare seared right through me.

I am invisible!

Did you know the first bicycle was called the hobbyhorse?

The day begins to heat up. Stubby whiskers itch and scratch my skin. I need to shave, but I've been too lazy here of late.

Possibly tomorrow!

What day is it?

Your Friend,
Jack Monroe

Dear Susan,

I just finished reading a book by an author whom I've read before. I must admit, the second one isn't as good as the first. Do you think most writers only have one spectacular book in them, and the rest are just so-so? I mean, look at Ayn Rand. *Fountainhead* was good, but *Atlas Shrugged* wasn't as great. Well, at least in my opinion.

Plus, that guy who wrote *Catcher in the Rye*. I can't think of his name right now, but I do know it begins with J.D.. Damn, that annoys me when I can't remember something so simple as a man's name.

I've been getting annoyed with myself a lot lately.

Salinger! J.D. Salinger. Can't remember what the initials stand for, but I know it's his name. My brain must have melted in the heat. How could I forget the author of *Catcher in the Rye*?

I shouldn't be getting down on myself, but it's built into my hard-drive, and I don't know how to get rid of these negative thoughts. Even when life seems great, and I'm doing things I want to be doing, there's always some anger brewing in me. Like I shouldn't be feeling this way, it's not natural, and then I don't.

The good light mood gone in an instant.

Man!

See, there I go again. I start out talking about books, and I fall into whining about my idiosyncrasies. I'm my own worst enemy, as the phrase goes.

Susan, do you think all humans are just host bodies for another species? You know, containers for an alien race stranded on our planet? And the only way they can survive is to live inside of our organic vessels? What a great sci-fi book!

Anywho!

Did you know Beavers can hold their breath for forty-five minutes?

I wish I could hold my breath that long. Hell, after sixty seconds I'm gasping for air. I don't have the lungs, or the will power. The thought of not breathing scares me a little. That is not how I want to die, not being able to breathe, like being trapped underwater as you fall through the ice trying to save your dog.

Could you imagine the terror, trying to find your way out, banging on the frozen water from below, watching the sun ripple the impenetrable ice, everything blurring above you? Your body begins to lose feeling as the frigid water freezes your blood, everything goes numb, your tightened lungs ache as they try to hold the last air. You exhale, knowing your next breath will be wet with death.

How horrific!

I was thinking maybe you might want to take a drive up into the mountains on Friday. We can meet at the plaza, get some lunch on the fly, and cruise up to the ski basin. Maybe hike up Mount Baldy. How does that sound?

Let me know?

I tell you, I've never been bitten by so many noseeums. My whole body is covered with these hard mounds, in which infecting venom is seeping into my blood. Just thinking about it gives me the creeps. A couple of the welts are scabbed over from me scratching at them so intensely.

Did you know there are 18 different animal shapes in the animal cracker zoo?

Funny facts, aren't they? I should maybe lay off the Snapple for a while, my waist line seems a little larger. Am I repeating myself? For the life of me I can't remember. Geeze, I tell you, my memory is really getting worse. Then there's that Salinger thing.

I miss Hazel Park. It's not much of a city, only around 10,000 people—two square miles by two square miles. At times it feels like a 2x2 square foot box. A quaint, uneventful, Detroit suburb. Except during the '68 riots. The neighborhood was never the same after that summer. I remember a friend's sister got raped when an unknown man entered their unlocked home and she was alone.

Andresen Ct. residents were furious, and the fury trickled down to us kids. I can still see myself, baseball bat in hand, screaming at the top of my lungs that I'd kill anyone who came onto our street. I was nine and had no real idea what was going on; I just felt the fear surrounding me.

After that summer, Dad insisted we start locking the doors, home or not.

Funny how violence changes the innocent.

I smell bacon frying. I be achin' for some bacon!

Did you know Lake Superior is the world's largest lake?

I love the Great Lakes, and I've seen all five.

I love Michigan. What a wonderful state. Fresh water surrounding the mitten shaped peninsula. Lush green lands filled with fresh scented air, like the first day of creation. I'm not talking about the large cities, but when you get away from Urbania, you'll know what I'm talking about.

I can't wait to get back.

Here, in Santa Fe, everything smells dusty, the inside of my nose is dried and caked with green crap. Sometimes I can barely breathe through my nostrils. I miss the Lake gulls, too, circling in the air currents. Around, here, in The City Different, all I see are huge ravens strutting their stuff, or sitting on fence posts like they were keeping guard of a fort. Their shiny, tar-black feathers gleam in the bright sunlight. I catch a dark eye filled with a mischievous glee. His broad shoulders give him a gangster effect. I wonder if he was part of the murder I witnessed this morning as a flock of crows flew above me?

I like this free flowing writing thing I'm doing. Just letting whatever comes to my mind coat these pages. Maybe, if you've been saving all these letters, you can make a book out of them. Maybe call it *The Suicide Letters of Jack Monroe.* That's kind of a catchy title, don't you think, Susan?

Okay, I'm just being stupid.

Did you know a sneeze travels out of your mouth at one hundred miles per hour?

Do I remind you of Cliff Clavin on "Cheers"? He was always pondering insignificant trivia. I found some of it interesting, but wasn't sure what was true or false. I guess these facts are true, otherwise they wouldn't be printed on those bottle caps.

I think I'm going to go sit by the window and watch the sunset!

I'm sorry I keep evading the answer to your question, but I still don't know what else I can do for you. I'll keep thinking.

Your Friend,
Jack Monroe

MID-
AUGUST

Dear Susan,

It's tomorrow!

I am so tired, I should just lie down and go back to sleep. It feels like I took a pill last night, but I know I didn't. It must have been the burger I ate from The Cowgirl Hall of Fame, a popular restaurant right down the street. The meal was huge, and I devoured the whole cow. Probably put myself into a food coma.

I've made a decision, Susan. If you don't meet me on Friday, I'm going to return to Michigan on Saturday. I'll drive back. It'll be good for me to take a road trip after such a disappointing experience.

As for this rental apartment, it's a week to week arrangement, so there'll be no problem here.

Don't get me wrong, Susan. I still care about you, and hope for the best. I'm just getting tired of the "one minute you need me, the next you don't." That's why it's important to show some good faith and rendezvous as planned; then I might be more inclined to believe your pleas.

The wall lamps rattle as a truck passes under my window.

Moisture dampens the air; the haze is humid. I'm reminded of the Midwest. One of those balmy, sweaty days where the sun stays behind the clouds, beaming into them, turning the afternoon into a sauna.

Anywho!

Dr. Who?

The other night, at least I think it was the other night, I was watching the news, and they had this story on about how a composer has come up with a solution for the ravaging, highly destructive bark beetle. He studied the beetles for a decade listening to their sounds and then figuring out what they meant.

So using vibrations to mimic their language, the composer designed a frequency that paralyzes the female in the mating chamber, and the male, thinking she's dead, starts to devour her. See, there's that vibration theory again, and if they can do it to insects, just think what they can do to people.

The world scares me, Susan!

Things are pretty fracked up and nobody seems to give a damn.

(Sorry about the swearing!)

Anyway, let's change the subject.

How are you?

You know, Susan, the more I think about your dilemma, the more I believe you should consider drug therapy. It's the latest craze now, prescription drugs. Every other advertisement on TV is for some kind of pill to cure some kind of ailment. The medicine doesn't heal you; it just numbs your symptoms, while your disease runs rampant. Does anybody else see what's wrong with this picture? Duh!

The ads really beginning to bug me are those for sex enhancement. Give me a break! If you can't get it up, there's a reason. Has anyone stopped to think about the long range consequences of these potions. Medicated, that's what we are, doped up and dumbed down.

Did you hear about the guy who got a Viagra stuck in his

throat and had a stiff neck for a week?

Susan, let me ask you a question. You might think it's really far out, but I'm curious.

Have you ever entertained the idea of killing someone? I mean, planned it out, detail by detail, on how you would do it, you know, and by what manner.

I have!

Many times!

Not that I would actually go through with it. Truth is, I just don't have the killer instinct in me. I mean, if harm was going to be brought to me, then, of course I would defend myself.

That's a whole other thing!

I think I would go for a juggler vein, because once the blood starts flowing, there's no going back. Plus, you know if you cut in the right place, it's a sure thing. Am I sick or what?

Anyway, maybe I should change the subject.

Did you know the Hummingbird's heart beats 1400 times a minute?

Sometimes I feel like I was born in the wrong era. Am I a few decades too late, and my time to shine is in the past?

So the best part of the year draws near. The beginning of football season. Being a die hard *Lions* fan, it's sometimes difficult to see the excitement of the games. Maybe this year will be the *miracle* year!

Are you a follower?

I've watched the sport since I was a kid. I'd hang out with Dad on Sundays, resting on my haunches in front of the set, rooting for those kitties. The Lions' blue and silver uniforms looked like gray/gray on the bubbled black and white TV sitting in the living room.

Then the ceiling came caving in when Mom killed herself. After that, football lost its meaning to Dad, and at the age of twelve, I was watching the games down at Charlie's Starting Gate, the nearest neighborhood bar. Charlie felt sorry for me, so he pretended not to notice the dark shadow sitting in the back corner, peering through grated shelves.

I'll never forget the stale, dingy, smells of cigarettes and sweaty, lonely men, gathering around a shit-hole, getting drunk on one dollar drafts, while cheering for a team whose fate you knew was inevitable. Last in the league.

Your Friend,
Jack Monroe

Dear Jack,

I'm in my backyard now, tiny Japanese fanned leaves wisp by me in the winds. I wish I could go somewhere, be alone with my craziness. I don't even know why I'm dragging you into this, it's not your burden.

I know you think I'm blowing you off by not meeting you, but I don't want to go out, away from my apartment. Why won't you come here? I think you'd like my place.

Last night I woke up screaming into my pillow. I have no idea what I was dreaming, but I'm sure it wasn't good. Today my nerves are a little on edge. I feel like I need to go for a walk, or a drive or something, but I'm afraid I might turn.

I'm really pissed off, Jack, livid with this being who's residing within me without my permission. I can't even move freely any longer, I'm dictated by her will, and I don't know how to break it.

My situation is dire!

A bee just landed on my arm, kissed my skin, and flew off!

Jack, are you still with me?

Am I driving you away?

I hope not, because I don't know what I'd do if I knew you weren't there.

I'm losing hope, Jack. Things just don't seem to matter anymore. My dreams and aspirations about life are nonexistent, and the thought of doing what I'm doing for the rest of my days does not inspire me.

Especially now that my Doppelganger has come to life.

What else can I refer to her as?

Your Friend,
Susan Jordan

Dear Susan,

I feel awful!

Yesterday after I wrote you, I decided to go for a walk. I went out through my secret hiding place, and strolled down to the plaza. I sat down on the nearest bench. As I was sitting there, this guy comes up and, towering over me, starts screaming that I had no business treating him the way I did, and how he wished I were dead.

Now come on, I've never seen this man before in my life. I jumped up and ran, only glancing back once to see if he was following me, but there was no one there. He'd disappeared. My heart was pounding; I thought for sure I was going to have a cardiac arrest.

Hurrying back to the rental, I decided to return the way I came, for fear if I were seen, questions might be asked of me about my tousled appearance. My breath was heavy and quick as I unlocked the brown wood door, and fell into the cool/dark living room.

I shook all over. This wet, clammy feeling coated my skin, and for a minute or two, I was afraid I was going to pass out. I didn't though. I stayed right where I was until the dizziness wore off.

I have no idea what to think of all of this. I mean, the guy seemed like he had a home, granted he was a little grungy, but a lot of people dress that way now-a-days for the sake of fashion. Something I'll never understand. Anyway, he just started yelling. Course, when reminiscing, it's kind of funny, as I believe he thought I was someone else. I suspect he was crazy.

Did you know it takes about ten billion mathematical calculations to predict one day's weather forecast?

I wonder what it all adds up to?

Do you think as we get older we forget how fragile life is because we're just so tired of living?

Did you know caller ID is illegal in California?

Your Friend,
Jack Monroe

Dear Susan,

Wow, do you think I'm crazy or what, writing all of these letters? I gaze out my window. Early autumn skies of cantaloupe oranges and daisy yellows blaze in my eyes, swelling the orbs with pools of tears.

I'm feeling a little sensitive. Must be my hormones. I am around the age they start to change, right?

Susan, Susan, the phone just rang, scaring the living shit out of me. My heart is pounding out of control, I feel like I'm having an anxiety attack, or worse, a heart attack. What if I die right here, nobody would know? You're the only person I've confided in as to my whereabouts, and I never see you. The woman who owns the place would come home and find my decomposing body lying here on the tiled floor. A foul stench in the air.

The caller didn't leave a message. I wonder if it was *that* Judith woman? I'll have to keep a closer eye out on things. How could she have gotten your/my number?

Now, I'm rattled Susan. I had been thinking about going for a walk after I finished writing you this letter, but now, I don't know. What if she's out there watching the apartment from her car. I did hear one pull up earlier and park, but I never heard a door open and close!

I wish you were here!

My heart sinks lower each and every moment I spend alone, sinking deeper into a cold foreboding hole. Frozen waters ice around me. My sight turns blurry, violet ripples swim in front of my eyes, pooling in chilled lids, freezing into tiny drops of liquid silver.

A car alarm blares in the distance, the evening is getting chilly after another scorcher of a day. At least the nights cool off quite considerably, so it is easier to sleep. I've been resting a lot better since moving out of the hotel. Not as much silent noise here.

Susan, do you think I've become emotionally obsessed with you, and have forgotten what this whole situation is about?

I'm here to try and help you make the right decision about your upcoming suicide, whether you should or shouldn't. I've been doing my part, keeping in touch with you day after day, for weeks now. You must realize I care?

I guess not!

Did you know the Starfish is the only animal that can turn it's stomach inside out?

Sometimes I feel like a motherless child.

Guess what—I am!

You know, Susan, people always harp about who we've hurt, but does anyone actually recognize those we've helped, even if we never know the impact of our words or gestures? Isn't that what counts?

Hey, here's what we can do. Let's make a separate list of the nice things we think we've done for people, and then we can compare them. I'm going to need all my concentration for this game.

I'll get back to you!

Your Friend,
Jack Monroe

Dear Susan,

I'm upset!

I think this whole arrangement is blowing up in my face. My mind is on the verge of snapping. I don't know what to do anymore.

Do you even care?

I'm beginning to think not!

I really believed I could have helped you.

Your Friend,
Jack Monroe

Dear Susan,

Oh, my gosh, I had a total meltdown, I am so sorry!
Will you ever forgive me?

Your Friend,
Jack Monroe

Dear Jack,

I'm feeling a little better today, not as jazzed up. I've been trying to meditate, capture my mind in a soft setting, relaxed and calm. Today, I stay indoors, the wind and occasional splashes of rain makes the backyard unappealing.

Jack, I believe the best thing I can do for myself is try to stay focused on maintaining my consciousness, because I think she invades me at those moments when I'm daydreaming, or thinking of something else, or when I'm off guard. Yeah, that's it, that's when this demon becomes me.

Am I rattling on?

Could be, I haven't talked to anyone in weeks, I have nothing to say, afraid I might spill the fact that I'm scared out of my wits, and I don't know what to do, and the only help out there is help that can't help me.

Does that make sense?

Jack, I'm glad you're my friend, I don't know what I'd do if I had to go through this alone.

Your Friend,
Susan Jordan

Dear Susan,

I've decided to leave Santa Fe and go home to Hazel Park. Go back to the familiar and comfortable. Try to forget this terrible time, the scenes, the beauty…you. Do you think I can, truly, ever rid my mind of our association? Would I want to? But my heart can do no more. I've tried to find an answer to your condition, and I only see one alternative.

Anyway, I don't want to get on the subject.

I tried this Chai Latte today. The taste was delicious, all smooth and milky, with dashes of cinnamon, ginger, and other exotic spices. Have you ever had one? I think you would like it. Maybe, if you're ever in Detroit you'll have to call me and I'll take you out for one.

Did you know Camels and Emus can't walk backwards?

I'm trying to figure out why I get so angry with you. I can feel it burn. Maybe it's not anger as much as frustration.

I think you should leave little traps to catch this woman you think is controlling you.

Maybe a camera is a good idea. I don't know. I guess I could help you set one up. That way you can see when you come and go, and maybe recognize this other being inside your mind. Then once we capture this imposter, we'll get rid of her.

Did you know Elephants are the only mammal that can't jump?

So much for an all-elephant basketball team!

The night is quiet, Susan. If I stop writing and listen real close, I can hear the heart-beat of the apartment, or is that mine? Or both? Have I been here so long I'm beginning to have the same pulse as these walls?

Come on, *Jack*, stop babbling!

The air outside is stormy calm. I see lightning flash above the dark mountain skyline. Did I ever tell you how I once almost got struck by lightning? Instead of hitting me, it jolted the mighty oak I was standing next to. Split the ancient tree down the middle, no splinters, like a laser sword of light. Misty smoke rose out of the embers' heart like the agonizing tears of a widowed bride.

Oh shit! Oops, sorry, but I just remembered this dream I had last night, and I gotta tell you this one, it was so weird. Anywho, *I'm at this party of a friend, whom I don't know, but it seems like we are pretty close. It is his birthday and all his friends and family are in attendance. I'm standing there, kind of bored, because even though I'm supposed to know all these people, I know no one. This guy comes up to me. I think he's catering the party. He has a chef's uniform on and asks me if I'd like to try a pickled jalapeno laced with acid. At first I think he's nuts, but then I look down and see he's holding the pepper between his fingers by the stem. I watch a spicy drop of juice hits the blonde sand on the ground. Should I or shouldn't I? is the question running around in my brain. I know the come down will be horrific. You know, the older you get, the more-timely the recovery. With little hesitation, I bite like a fish at a fly and gobble the chile down, choking on the hot flavor. I stand here for quite a while, waiting for the drug to take effect, but there is nothing. I walk over to where my friend is, but he's engaged in conversation with these people whose faces are melting. I begin laughing loudly, and turning, I run down these railroad tracks. Everything is dark, and the night is freezing, even though it is July. I walk so far I don't know where I am anymore. I see a slow moving cart, being pulled by a moped as an old Asian man with a scraggly white beard straddles the seat. Jogging unnoticed up behind it, I jump on the back, and crouching down on my knees, notice what resembles two dead bodies wrapped in these stained white shrouds. One is the size of a small child. I am horrified. I can't scream because I don't want the driver to see me. I place my hand over my mouth as I see red and white stars sparkling in front of me. I think I'm going to throw up as I gag myself with my hand. The jostling of the cart doesn't help. I kept telling myself I'm having a bad trip.*

Then, I woke up!

Crazy, huh!

What do you think?

Maybe it has something to do with my own mother's death, and when she died, so did I, or at least a part of me. You know what I mean, right?

As expected, I was quite freaked out when I awoke, and was unable to get back to sleep. I've been awake for a long time now. Well over 18 hours.

See, Susan, I can't stay mad at you. If you weren't in my life, who would I be able to share these psychotic dreams with?

Your Friend,
Jack Monroe

Dear Jack,

I thought you were adapting to Santa Fe, or at least that's the impression I got from you, so I was surprised when I read you intended to go back to Hazel Park. I'm sorry you get mad and frustrated with me. Think how I feel, split apart, living two lives, not knowing what kind of person my other half is; will she hurt me, is she nice, funny, or dark and devilish.

Jack, I need to tell you this, but make sure you don't share it with anyone else. I think she wants me dead as much as I her. I truly believe she wants to take over my being totally. What if she succeeds, will she inhabit my soul too?

Things are getting out of hand Jack, and yes, I do think hiding a camera is a good idea. I know exactly where to put it. I won't tell you right now, she might be listening.

Jack, I want to know who this *thing* thinks she is. Invading me, not even having the consideration to ask first. Who knows, I might have said yes freely if I would have gotten to know her first.

But now it's war!

I sit in a pile of dust, Jack, my desk is covered with finger printed dirt. It's been so long since I've written that my yellow legal pads are coated gray. I can see lines drawn through the ash checking the depth of the accumulation. Pretty soon I'll need a pole to measure the footage.

Is this what my life has come too? Replaying past lives, those never to happen again. How many times do I wish to relive a certain year, day, hour. Please, fate, I beg you, just let me experience that feeling one more time.

Are those regrets, Jack?

Do you think?

Your Friend,
Susan Jordan

Dear Susan,

I'm so thirsty, and I've run out of Snapple! I hate water, never have liked the taste of it. Even though people say there is no flavor, there is. Water tastes like *water*!

I should go out and find one of those 24-hour gas stations; surely they'd have something to quench my dry tongue. I tell you, Susan, I think the drink I love best when I'm parched is an ice cold glass of apple cider. The tangy crisp juice, sweet when it hits the back of the tongue. A rich amber nectar filled with satisfying sensations.

When I was a child, every fall our school class would take a field trip to Yates Cider Mill, about 30 minutes from Hazel Park. They milled the best cider I have ever tasted. What fond memories! The sky autumn blue, and the air smelling of dying wet leaves, as a cool Halloween breeze brushes my cheek. I always feel a sense of freedom at that moment, like everything will be all right.

I still go every year, but I don't think I'll make it this season. The time is drawing near for the apples to be just right, but my work here is not done yet. I'll stay for you, help you try to get rid of this alien inside of you. Then I must go, I grow weary of the City Different.

Maybe I'm just getting old and home bound.

Did you know that before they used Mercury in ther-mometers, they used brandy?

Do you know what's funny, Susan? When I first started corresponding with you, I didn't realize it was going to be so difficult, and yes at times, especially at the beginning when you wouldn't contact me, I began to lament this arrangement.

But I see now this letter writing therapy is working.

You're finally facing your demon, wanting to rid yourself of her. Between the two of us, she doesn't stand a chance.

That's why I'm staying. If I stop now, you just might kill yourself!

Did you know the average snail weighs seven hundred and sixty nanograms?

Whatever a nanogram is!

You know, Susan, sometimes I just want to get in my car and drive. Never look back. Find a small cabin somewhere, make it my own, and live off the land. Disappear into nature and never be seen or heard from again. A kind of Thoreau-like existence.

Maybe that's what you should do instead of killing yourself. Just run away. What's the difference? People will still be hurt. But that way you can continue to enjoy and appreciate all of the beauty life has to offer us.

I do believe life is the most wonderful dream of the entire universe. Being able to experience such diversity, to smell an apricot tree blooming in April, to hear rushing rivers tumble over moss-coated rocks.

I don't know, maybe I'm getting off the subject at hand, but still, when you look right at it, life is pretty damn good. Embrace it! Do I sound like a fanatic? Hope not!

Did you know the pupils of our eyes expand forty-five percent when looking at something pleasing?

Makes sense to me, my eyes always enlarge when I see you. (Just kidding!)

I hear tom-tom drums in the background. The beat is a very mystical rhythm; it soothes my soul.

Your Friend,
Jack Monroe

Dear Susan,

The sky looks ominous. Dark rain clouds cover every inch of space, and low rumbles echo off the black hills. The air is quiet, trying not to make a sound, hoping to remain unseen, unheard, unknown. Kind of like me. At times I wish I were invisible. Just walking through life like a vapor.

Maybe I need to go out and make more friends. But why? I really don't enjoy spending my free time with people.

I suppose I have companion issues, really don't want to get close to anyone.

Until you!

I guess I have found the perfect job, though. Writing suicide letters on behalf of those contemplating this final act of freedom.

I've pretty much been alone since my arrival to this fair city of Santa Fe, and it's kind of grown on me. Still, I may be liking it more because I know I'm going to be leaving soon.

There's no way I could spend the rest of my life here.

Anyway, I once again got off the subject. But the bottom line is, I don't want to go out and make new friends.

I have enough!

You'll do just fine!

We are friends, aren't we, Susan?

I mean, I've been telling you a lot of personal stuff about me, things I wouldn't dare tell anyone else. So, that in itself constitutes a friendship, right?

Golly, I love you!

Do you believe in a higher-power, Susan? You know,

someone or some mysterious entity you believe is there for you, and will always be by your side through thick and thin, whatever one conceives that entity to be.

I do!

Just knowing I'm not alone and that no matter what happens, things will work themselves out, comforts me.

I once read the true meaning of enlightenment is when one accepts the knowledge of a higher-power.

So!

Do you go to church, Susan?

I used to. I was baptized a Catholic, traumatized at an early age, for what? How could I commit such a mortal sin when I was just born? Who am I to take on the guilt of others?

I'm not Christ, nor have I ever claimed to be. I'm getting sick, Susan, sick of this world and all the jerks who run it. Will somebody please set us free?

I remember, as a child, having to go to Mass. I hated it. No matter what, as soon as I got there, I had to pee, but we were always late, so Mom made me wait until the end before I could go.

One Sunday, I just couldn't hold it, and as the lambs marched up to the sacrificial altar for the body and blood of Christ, I urinated all over the kneeler and floor. I can still see the silver-green oil slick forming right under Mr. Gutch's shoe. A sour stench rose from my undershorts. Before I knew it, Mom was yanking me out of the pew, dragging me and my pair of pee-soaked pants down the center of the aisle. She stared straight ahead, while I walked like a sailor, shifting my weight back and forth from the cooling wetness. I had to wear a diaper to church every Sunday from then on out. I was 9, and the bulge of the thick cloth undergarment gave me rosy cheeks for the rest of my life.

Did you know you could cover San Francisco with all the water contained in US swimming pools?

Your Friend,
Jack Monroe

Dear Susan,

I was awakened by a knock at my door this morning. Thinking it might be you, I jumped out of bed, tripping on the covers and smacking my forehead on the hardwood floor. A knot arose. I've had a splitting headache ever since. I don't mind the injury, what bothers me is when I got to the door, no one was there.

Was it you?

Why didn't you wait?

Didn't you hear me call out?

Oh, gosh, Susan, if I missed you again, I'm going to kill myself.

This can't be happening. I don't understand.

Did I scare you off, was my voice too harsh, too brash? Please, for Pete's sake, answer me!

Your Friend,
Jack Monroe

Dear Jack,

Where are you? I've been waiting for your response as to whether or not you'll help me install the video camera I bought. I haven't heard neither hide nor hare from you.

What's going on?

It's funny, the other night I was listening to the distant sounds coming from downtown and I wished I had your phone number, because I would have called you to see if you wanted to take a stroll, see what all the ruckus is about. I'm getting lonely!

Anywho, I managed to install the camera myself. I concealed the tiny device in the corner above the front door. I can practically see every inch of the living room and kitchen.

I'll run it for a week or so to see how many times my imposter comes out.

Don't ask me what I'm going to do after that, okay? I do not have an answer.

Susan Jordan, PI!

I'm beginning to lose my belief in magic, Jack!

Do you think everything we see and believe is one big illusion, and when we die we're released from this schizophrenic four-gray-walled prison?

In a way I'm breaking free from the hologram, changing the frequency of the vibrations controlling me, splitting apart from the evil within, liberating my soul from the blackened demons forever tormenting me.

Am I not rich with faint desires of harmony and bliss?

Do I not possess the powers to present myself with these gifts?

Or the strength to take them away.

It is I, who will decide my fate.

Not the gods or goddess who lied when they said they'd watch out for me.

Nor Satan and his idle-handed devils.

I have committed no crime. My punishment and imprisonment is unjustified.

I demand a new trial.

Life, liberty and the pursuit of happiness. *Cacca Toro!*

Did you know the first soap opera debuted on TV in 1946?

I found one of your Snapple bottle caps.

Your Friend,
Susan Jordan

Dear Susan,

Let me tell you about my hardest client. Her name was Nadine. When she contacted me, her one and only daughter had just been raped and murdered in Miami while vacationing with old friends. She was fifteen.

Nadine was devastated, tried a couple of times to kill herself, but unsuccessfully. The woman concluded she wasn't able to do the act because she needed a closure, a letter expressing how she felt and the why's of her decision.

I completed several drafts for her, but nothing was ever right. Finally, she gave up on me, and conveyed that she had changed her mind about the whole suicide business, and that she was going to try and muster up the courage to continue on with life.

Nadine didn't make it too far. Six months later she was successful with her murder, and the only words she left were on a square of toilet paper which read, *Good-bye*!

Funny, aye!

Poor Nadine!

Your Friend,
Jack Monroe

Dear Susan,

I'm sick, sicker than a dog. I must've eaten something really bad because I can't keep anything down, I don't know what to do!

Please, calm me, think of me. Do something. If I vomit one more time, I believe my insides will fall out. I've been drinking bottle after bottle of water, and shoving saltine crackers down my throat. Nothing's working.

I'm scared!

I've been sweating all night, soaking my sheets with perspiration. Shivers race over me, rippling every raw nerve of my hot/cold body. My temperature fluctuates back and forth, up and down. One second I'm ablaze with fever, the next, chilled dead to the bone.

I want to call for help, but I'm afraid they'll take me to the hospital, and then I'd miss our visit. I so look forward to seeing you. I've never been so in tune with someone as I am with you. I truly think we're at the point where we could read each other's minds.

Maybe?

Maybe not!

Last night, I was so exhausted and depressed I cried. Bawled like a baby. My whole body shook with unforgiving sobs. My throat raged red, seared by hacking, dry coughs. There were no angels on my bedpost last night.

And none when I awoke this morning!

To say the least, I *am* starting to feel better, although I'm still very weak. I think I've been ill for three days now. The bedroom smells of mildew, aging mucus. Makes me want to gag. I need to get rid of this stench before the owner returns.

Hey, Susan, I'm sorry. I've been so wrapped up in myself lately, it seems like I've forgotten about you. How are things? Any progress on locating your Doppelganger? Will you have the guts to kill your demon when you find her?

For your sake, I hope so!

Life is too precious to throw it away.

Maybe when you do find your squatter, the two of you can figure something out so that neither one of you has to die. Because you know if one goes, the other will too.

Did you ever think of that scenario?

I'm starting to feel a spring-like sensation that always passes through me when I'm sick. It's a warm day in February, or a cool one in July. You know the feeling, right?

Anywho, I'm boring you, aren't I? And don't lie, because I've dulled myself.

I open the window, and a breath of cool morning air washes over my fevered body. My eyes water from the sudden dryness. I step back, sideswiping brown dirt as it blows past me. I hear tiny pebbles ping against the mirror.

The wind halts!

The drapes are still against the chipped/white window frame. A tiny flutter disturbs the calm, like a ghost fleeting through. I am at ease now. The spirit has fled.

It's funny how I've suddenly become depressed. I don't recall at any time in my past life getting so emotionally down, as I am here in New Mexico. What is it?

I know what you're thinking, and, no, it's not you. Don't even go there. You're the best thing that has ever happened to me, can't you see that? Just think how worse our lives would be if I didn't know you.

Of course, if I didn't know you, I wouldn't be in Santa Fe.

That's neither here nor there.

I'm where I'm supposed to be, and there is no doubt in my mind!

Your Friend,
Jack Monroe

Dear Jack,

The other day I went up to my bedroom, and there was this awful smell. I don't know where it came from, and was thinking maybe a skunk or raccoon was lying dead somewhere in the acre of land behind my apartment.

It's gone now, and I wonder if maybe my senses are starting to play tricks on me.

I don't know how much longer I'm going to be able to take this insanity. My assassin's infiltrating closer now, Jack. I believe she's reading your letters. We should start communicating telepathically, so she won't know what we're planning.

I know it won't be easy, but I truly believe it is the best route.

There's a big fire up near Los Alamos. I guess the lab is threatened and the whole town has been evacuated. The skies are strawberry red, and with rain smoke. Huge clouds form above, towering 30,000 feet. Plumes of burning ash. The air is surreal; a vanilla haze floats in the foothills.

I can taste the tragedy on my tongue. Reminds me of charred chicken!

I should be scared, but am not, thinking maybe Mother Nature will help with my dilemma, and I can take the easy way out.

Maybe I should go find a hot spot, and jump into the inferno.

Your Friend,
Susan Jordan

SEPTEMBER

Dear Susan,

I am so much better than the last time I wrote to you. I feel like a new man now. I took a long hot shower, cleaned myself up, brushed my teeth, aired out the apartment, and put on some fresh clothes.

Autumn rustles in the trees. Aging leaves crackle against each other, calling out to the goblins and beasts: Come forth ye demons, the Day of the Dead draws near. Nostalgia springs within me.

I've made a decision, Susan. Now that the delirium of the fever has passed, I can once again think coherently and rationally. What I've decided is, I'll give this experiment three more weeks, by then if we can't come to an understanding, I will return to Michigan. No holds barred.

Whatever that means!

I'm serious, Susan, I'm not joking around this time. I know there have been times in the past when I've made the same threat, but this time *Ma Cherie*, take it to heart, I will leave.

I'm beginning to feel like I'm wasting my time. Nothing I do seems to work. I try to figure out what is wrong with you, even thought you might have Psychogenic Fugue Syndrome. It's a state where the person loses time and senses, doesn't recall anything after they come back. Kind of like what you're experiencing.

I found out about fugues on one of those CSI TV programs. So, I went to the library to research more information about it, realizing this might be your problem. After reading the symptoms, I came to the conclusion that it's unlikely you suffer from this syndrome. I mean, even though you're affected by personality confusion, and as far as you know, have taken on another identity, there are too many missing elements to have you fall under this category.

People suffering from fugues usually only experience one black out, not several as you do. Unless of course you've suffered a trauma, or severe depression, something along those lines, then we might want to look into this more.

Sorry! I'd hoped we could have put a name to your illness, make it more familiar to us so it doesn't seem so foreign.

Do you think there's an alien fungus eating our brains?

Now, Susan, ponder this thought. I know I mentioned it before, but why do you think people get so angry sometimes, some on a snap. I believe this species sends out mico- toxins, and they stimulate certain parts of your brain, usually the anger area.

Doesn't that make sense?

What do you mean, "Stop talking crazy!" You know I'm not. Hey listen, just because I agreed to this telepathy angle doesn't mean you can use it for snide remarks. You're starting to piss me off.

Did you know the U.S. Coast Guard uses trained pigeons to find people lost at sea?

PBR is playing some George Winston this morning. His haunting music touches me like a kiss of mist upon my cheek.

I sometimes wish I knew how to play an instrument, but I've never been inclined to actually do so. Plus, I don't think I have the discipline to practice all the time. Then there's a thing called *talent*, of which I seem to be bereft.

Your Friend,
Jack Monroe

Dear Susan,

Earlier I meandered downtown, dusk rose from the pale sky. The plaza was lined with white tents. It reminded me of an army camp. Fiestas are beginning, a big week-long festival to celebrate the Spanish conquering of Santa Fe. How appropriate that the set-up reminds me of a military encampment.

I guess also, there's the *Burning of Zazobra*. A huge papier-mâché doll, about sixty feet tall, (not positive about the height, but he's tall, really tall) shaped like a man that they burn every year to be rid of doom and gloom. It's a big tradition here in Santa Fe. Maybe I should go check it out, get rid of some of my gloom and doom.

The air smells like roasting corn and burning meat. Hoots and howls ring out through the bright night, faint bells careen off the crowd's noise. My mouth waters as I get lost in the multitudes, searching for a carne taco.

Your Friend,
Jack Monroe

Dear Susan,

Oh, my dear, dear Susan. Listen to a poem I found on her desk, which by the way is dustier than the backyard. I know I shouldn't be snooping around, but this piece is so lovely, I wanted to share it with you:

Ebb Tide
I want love
no more.
I no longer
desire to
dive into it
swim through it,
drown beneath it.
My heart
has anchored
on broken shelled
shores,
water-logged
trees piled
haphazardly
against the
embankment,
washed to shore
by unforgiving
tides.
I walk on
cutting sands
of broken hearts
and tormenting
thoughts.

I wait
and watch
as ebb tide
approaches,
tempting me,
begging me,
to try love
just once more.

Isn't that fabulous?

I wish my writing was as peaceful. See, I do have a creative spirit, just no skill.

Maybe all I need to do is practice.

Do you feel lucky to have your talent, Susan? I'm sure you do. I bet your poetry is wonderful. I can tell. What, with your confidence and sense of humor, I'm sure your artistic spark shines.

Hopefully you'll let me read some of your poems one day!

I want to apologize, Susan, for the harshness of my last letter. Sometimes there's this strange sensation in my brain, and it gets me angry. Then I think to myself: Why are you treating me like this? I mean, I have feelings, too, right? Shouldn't they be respected as I do yours?

I don't want to get into this right now. I'm in a good mood, and it feels like the virus has left me, so my outlook is rosy. What a blast, going from being deathly sick, to being in the pink. I cannot tell you how good I feel right now. Like I'm thirty again, and my dreams are still in the believable stage.

Have you ever experienced these sensations, Susan?

I'm sure you have. You can tell me all about it when we see each other.

Anywho!

Did you know there are 63,360 inches in a mile?

Fact!

You know, Susan, sometimes it's hard to come up with things to talk about. It feels like I'm communicating with a wall. I'm sure these letters would be much more interesting if it were a two-way conversation, instead of me just babbling on about nothing.

I know, I know, the few letters you've written me *are* something. You don't have to give me attitude. I just think it'd be nice to get a few more.

Do you know what I read in the paper today? Well, I'm sure you're aware of the state of the economy. Detroit is so bad off that they've come up with an idea to turn their neighborhoods into farmland. Tear down all of the rat infested, abandoned houses and plant vegetables. New Age victory gardens.

I think it's a great plan. If they can come up with a way where the lands are co-opted, and the people work the fields for jobs, then it just might work. Michigan is a very fertile land. With all the water and sun it gets, I can see it happening!

Returning to the old, tried and true. Maybe that's what it will take.

Did you know honey bees use the sun to navigate?

Your Friend,
Jack Monroe

Dear Susan,

Last night, I was lying around, unable to sleep, and I thought about the poem I read/sent to you. Figured I'd get up and try my hand at it. Here's what came out.

Where Thunder Sleeps
Today,
and since the very
first day
I saw you,
looked into
your eyes,
shook your
hand good-bye.
I knew.

Since the beginning,
while thundering skies
creased red horizons,
melding them into
heaven and earth.
I knew.
As rain began
to fall,
dripping wet
on molten rock,
sculpting,
creatures,
beings,
into existence,
as blinding lightning

ripped at my soul.
I knew.

When caution flickered
in the gray,
revealing tumultuous journeys,
I continued to search
for the cavern
where thunder sleeps.
Quietly hoping to rattle
the dreams of heaven
and the blazing horizons.
It was then,
I knew.

Today,
and since the first
time
you saw me,
looked into my eyes,
shook my hand good-bye.
I knew.

I was thinking of you when these words soared into my mind. That's how I feel, and deep down, I truly believe you're experiencing the same thing.

So, Susan, what's your take? I mean, it's okay, right?

After all, *you* are the poet!

I tell you, it felt so good to write. As you know, jotting down your thoughts and feelings is very therapeutic. I always feel better after I draft you a letter.

My mood's pretty stable right now. Hang on a minute. I want to get another cup of hot Joe; there's a little chill in the air this morning.

I hear the java in my cup fizzling. I lean closer and listen—yup, it's sizzling all right. I figure it must be the cream and the coffee fusing. I lift the mug off its saucer and the vibration ceases.

I saw a little article in the paper this morning where a New Zealand woman sold two ghosts in bottles for a little over $2000. I wonder if they need to be certified ghost keepers in order to see the spirits? Or if the spirits are making the caretakers certified?

We live in such a crazy world! Don't you think so, too, Susan?

When I was a young boy, I used to daydream a lot in grade school. When it came to certain subjects, (Math, English, Science) the nuns just couldn't hold my attention. Anyway, I would design these wooden vehicles in my head. They would be wind and chain powered, with perfectly rounded wheels. You couldn't get anywhere fast, but at least you could get there in one solid piece.

I guess it makes perfect sense for a young boy from Detroit to think about building cars.

I hear this loud obnoxious sound coming down the street with a base booming like a dying man's heart. I look out the window, but see nothing. Is it in my chest? Is it my heart?

Mares eat oats, and Does eat oats, and little lambs eat ivy. A kid will eat ivy too. Wouldn't you?

Your Friend,
Jack Monroe

Dear Jack,

Things are getting worse. The blackouts are more frequent. Now, I'm waking up in the middle of the Plaza, or just walking down the street. The other day I came to, and found myself standing in the middle of St. Francis Drive during rush hour trying to get to the other side. I wasn't at a cross light either.

Talk about being terrified!

I can't take it anymore, Jack.

Do you ever hear her, Jack, I mean now that we've opened up telepathically, do you ever listen to her thoughts? What you can do is start concentrating on the times when she's me. You might be able to pick something up. I'm sure you can tell us apart. Then you can tell me what she's thinking.

Advantage, me!

I'm a mess, Jack, I can't stop shaking. The idea that I don't have control anymore is driving me to the edge.

I really need you now, Jack, please don't disappoint me, not this time, I can forgive you for all the other dashed hopes, but not now, please Jack, be here!

Your Friend,
Susan Jordan
P.S. Maybe I might have a form of fugues!

Dear Susan,

When the going gets tough, the tough get going!

When I was a boy, for a little while this friend of Dad's used to stop by every night.

Bill Hall was his name. He just popped in out of the blue, an old school chum of Dad's. Bill was always drunk on his ass. His body odor was so pungent Dad wouldn't let him in the house. The two would sit out on the steps of the front porch, swilling beers until Mom finally put her foot down and chased the bum away.

Those drunken evenings didn't last too long. Bill Hall disappeared as fast as he appeared.

The point of my story is he would always repeat that phrase whenever Dad answered the door. *When the going gets tough, the tough get going*! The saying has never made sense to me. Does it to you, Susan?

I can still see his sun burnt dirty face in the hallowed light of the night.

Poor man!

Do you think people are predestined to meet, Susan?

I do!

Not everyone though! Just those who are supposed to make a difference in each other's lives. Like you did for me. Before I met you, sure I was living, but just surviving. I had no dreams or goals or ambitions except to get through the next day.

Then, after you, I was energized. I came down to the southwest, and discovered an unusual beauty I had never imagined. Can you tell Santa Fe has grown on me? The city's mystical power reminds me of you.

What's your favorite nut?

For me, I'd have to say the pistachio. The only problem with them, though, is you can't eat just one, kind of like those Lays potato chip ads of days gone by. My favorite though, is just opening up a can of the Planters mixed nuts, and lying back on the couch with a coke and a good movie on the tube.

For me, that's life!

Did you know Camel milk doesn't curdle?

Be talking to you soon!

Your Friend,
Jack Monroe

Dear Susan,

I want to tell you what life's all about. Yesterday, as I started to do the dishes, I turned the faucet on without looking. Glancing down I realized I'd drowned a spider. My heart sank, as I studied its soaked legs, limp and lifeless. I tore off a square of paper towel from the roll and gently lifted the arachnid from its tiny puddle.

I set its limp body on the shelf above the sink, and watched with concern. One of its appendages rose in the air, and noticing I'd laid him on his back, quickly turned him upright. Staring with dread, I saw his legs beginning to stretch out, and figured the motion to be a good sign.

The sun was shining on the spot where he lay. My heart was pounding out of my chest. I felt so bad. I mean, I've killed spiders before, but there was something about this tiny creature making me surge with compassion.

I didn't want to sit like a bump on a log staring at him. I knew recovery time was necessary, so I bagged the dishes, and retreated to my bed, where I lay down to read. Curiosity tickled my judgment, however, and before I knew it, I was back at the sink, checking on my patient.

It didn't look good. His thread like legs curled beneath him, the way they do when a spider dies, or at least that's how they are when I find them dead in the garage. I wonder if humans were to die naturally, would their limbs curl up, too?

Anyway, I knew he was dead. I was so sad, Susan. You can't believe how this realization made me feel. I began crying, not sobbing, more like a whimper, but still, crying. I thought about flushing the remains down the toilet, but instead, walked away, and sat down to write you.

I forgot about the incident after a while, until I went to pour a glass of water. I flicked the light on, and glancing over at the ledge, remembered the spider immediately. The corpse was gone!

He lives!

I was ecstatic, my heart felt like it was going to jump out of my chest. I saved the tiny spider. What more could I ask?

That's what life's all about? Just when you think all hope has gone, it reappears.

I feel transformed, like my life has purpose, reason, tranquility. I don't think I'll ever kill another spider from here on out. I know I can do the same for you. I'm not using this as an analogy to persuade you to listen to me, or come running to my door. No, it's just a little story I thought you might like.

Don't get so defensive!

You know, sometimes you take things the wrong way!

Maybe you should listen before you react.

I hear tiny pings of sprinkling rain tapping against my window. It's been stormy for over a week now. At first, the coolness and drizzle were a comfort to me, but then after the third day, I was getting tired of it, and now on the sixth day, I am beginning to loathe the moisture.

What can I do?

The sky was pretty neat the other day. There was a double rainbow across the mountains. The ultra-violet lights of the multi-colored bow, sent shivers down my spine. It was spectacular! I don't get to see many rainbows back in Hazel Park. I forget how magical they are. Santa Fe sure is beautiful!

Do you believe in reincarnation, Susan?

Have I asked you this before?

You seem like the kind of person who would, because you're so at ease with the idea of killing yourself. So, you must believe in something, if you're willing to end your life in this realm.

Do you ever wonder why one toe-nail grows faster than the others?

Did I ever tell you about, Mr. Reiguer. He was this old German man who lived across the street from us. He had a big brick two story house, and a large yard, where Lumpy, his German Shepherd ran free. I used to ride Lumpy like a pony. I loved that dog.

One night I saw my father talking to Mr. Reiguer, and the next day he, his wife and Lumpy were gone. No one ever said anything about the disappearance, and a new family moved in a week later.

I never found out why they left so suddenly. I was sad, my friend Lumpy was gone, and so was the extra cash Mr. Reiguer would pay me when I'd crawl through the milk chute after he'd accidentally lock his keys in the house. I was a small child. When I was older, I began to wonder if maybe he was a German-Jew, who had escaped to the United States to hide out until WW II ended and it was safe to go back home.

All I know is he was a very nice man, and I'll never forget him or his German Shepherd, Lumpy.

Do you find it intriguing to think today could be the last day of your life? Nobody knows when they're going to die, well, save for death row convicts. *They* know! But, when you really sit down and think about it, Susan, it's very mysterious.

There's a lot to be said for the saying, *live today like it's your last day alive!*

Your Friend,
Jack Monroe

Dear Susan,

I just saw nine Ravens flying across the gray clad sky!

Macabre is in the air!

Be alert!

I'm thinking about going for a stroll downtown. I don't know why it comforts me so. Maybe we can meet somewhere. How about at the obelisk erected in the center of the plaza? I know this is short notice, but please, try to make it. It'd be so nice to see you, Susan. I'm sure it will be like old times. I'll buy you a fajita!

How about, tomorrow night, say six?

Trust me, I won't get mad if you don't show up. I know this is spontaneous, so I'll understand if you can't make it. All I ask is that you contact me and let me know if you can't. That way I won't waste my time going into the masses.

I'll send this letter off right now, so you get it in time.

Your Friend,

Jack Monroe

Dear Susan,

I'm back!

I went to mail this last letter you just received, and maybe by the time you get my note, we will have already seen each other.

Oh, happy day!

You know, Susan, I consider you my best friend.

I feel like I can tell you my woes and sorrows, joys and laughs. Is it all the same to you, as it is for me? There's a link between us fusing our minds. I can't describe it, or explain it. I only *feel* it.

Like we're soul mates!

We're one!

That's why it scares me when you talk about killing yourself, because if you die, then I die. And the only thing left after that is the empty shell of a man.

I need you, Susan! Please realize this.

You know, don't you?

No!

You're saying, *no*, you don't realize how much I depend on you?

I'm going to drop this subject right now, because the whole thing is upsetting me, and I don't want to loose the good mood I'm in.

Did you know strawberries are the only fruit that have their seeds on the outside?

There, the subject is changed!

Do you ever wonder, Susan, why humans aren't allowed to do what they love doing? Why are we in this hell hole trying to survive and being miserable about it? Honestly, how many people do you think are unhappy, discontented, dreading the rest of their lives if they have to live it the same way.

Isn't that how it goes, Susan?

You know it as well as I do, the answer is yes.

Your Friend,

Jack Monroe

Dear Jack,

I hate life right now!

I'm a prisoner in my own body. I'm too afraid of going out in public, and I'm so pissed off over this circumstance and the fact that there's only one option for help, and that's really of no help.

I'm getting closer to my execution, Jack. What's the point anymore? All I ever hear on the news are these depressing doomsday stories. I want to live in peace. You know, staying in the positive.

But it doesn't work that way, does it Jack?

You, yourself said, there's always a black cloud around, even when you're feeling good, right?

I'm fed up with my tenant. I want her out!

My life is over!

I have no more will, desire, expectations of a sunny horizon. Release me from this tormenting craziness I call life. I'll chew through the shackles cast around my emotions, setting free all the grace and joy buried deep within.

Am I truly not just a ball of energy in an organic form?

I'm sick, Jack, and there's no cure.

The sun sets over the Jemez Mountains. Streams of lavender and mahogany clouds dazzle the landscape. These are the things I'll miss, unless what I believe about death is true, and we sidestep into another dimension of sorts. I don't know. Who am I to think I can figure out the greatest mystery on earth.

Mystery, or secret, that is the question.

You know, Jack, the other day I found a Snickers wrapper in my trash and have no idea where it came from. Well, I do, kind of sort of. I don't eat crap like that, so it means my imposter is eating junk and probably doing things to my body I would never dream of.

Now do you see why I'm so freaked out? Put yourself in my shoes, Jack, how would you feel?

I hear a tree being shredded next door. What a way to go, mulched into pulp.

Nope, I want a softer, more gentle departure.

Would you like to come with me, Jack? We'll have a wonderful time together, and don't you think it might be easier dying with another? Someone you're compatible with?

Will you consider my proposal, Jack?

When I insisted we only use telepathy to communicate, I didn't realize how hard it would be. I mean, sometimes I can tap into you, but most of the time, I draw a blank.

It doesn't seem to be working.

Maybe it has to do with, *her*!

Probably sticking her big fat nose into our business again! *Bitch*!

The other day, Jack, I was sitting in the backyard, and the wind began howling. The umbrella I have up, started to blow away. As I grabbed the stand and held the tarp firm, I listened to the rain pounding sounds of the breezes ripping at the weak cloth. The drops were cold with ice, as gale forces tore at the canvas. I thought the parasol was going to split, as the cunning current whirled dirt devils in the air.

Sorry, I won't be able to meet you at the plaza, I'm afraid to go out.

Your Friend,
Susan Jordan

Dear Susan,

What day is it? Did I miss our meeting at the plaza? I don't know where I've been. I feel drugged, but I know I haven't taken anything. And there was no way of getting a Mickey slipped to me. I haven't been out of the apartment in days.

What happened?

I don't remember anything.

It's night time and I'm scared. I hear tambourines shimmering outside, my nerves jitter, sending goose bumps along my arms. My mouth is dry. I try to swallow, but ancient dust coats my throat.

I'm not who I am!

I'm not who you think I am!

I'm not even the person I used to be!

My mind is numb, intoxicated, full of this something I know I got caught in, but shouldn't have.

Your Friend,
Jack Monroe

Dear Susan,

I'm so sorry about my last letter, I kind of lost it. Somehow my time table got all screwed up and I thought it was tomorrow. Guess I slipped into a deep dream state. My mind was so garbled, kind of fluffy, like pink cotton-candy.

I can't believe I got so wigged out.

Anyway, another day! And I have recovered.

How are you, Susan?

Me, I'm feeling a little lonely, but I think today will be better.

Susan, I was thinking last night how different you are from my other friends. Those people are just occasional, go-have-a-beer-and-a-laugh-with buddies. There's no one I want to hang around with. Certainly not for long periods of time. That's probably another reason why I'm alone. I think I could hang out with you for a long time, though, and not be bugged by it.

Don't you feel the same?

I mean, we're so natural together, and we have a lot in common even though we're opposites.

You'll know what I'm talking about when I see you at the plaza, and speaking of such, I'm going to go get ready now, take a shower and head out!

See you there!

Your Friend,
Jack Monroe

Dear Susan,

That's it! I'm gone, outta here! Don't ever try to contact me again. What do you think I am, some jackass who's going to keep setting himself up to get kicked in the balls? Uh-huh, not me!

Day after day I've tried to reach out to you, to comfort you, give you all the advice and wisdom I felt you needed. But you just turned around and threw it back in my face. What am I supposed to think?

This time, this time is the bomb. The final detonation that will blow our whole relationship up in the air. You think I'm kidding? You're saying to yourself you've heard all this before, that I'll cool down in a day or two, and then things will get back to normal.

Well, you're wrong!

Your Friend,
Jack Monroe

MID-SEPTEMBER

Dear Susan,

I killed a black widow this morning. I didn't mean to. It was just a reaction. She startled me. The deadly creature was hanging upside down waiting for prey. I smashed it before her Majesty knew what happened. I guess that's the best way. Her black guts spread across the bathroom tile, almost making me throw up. I threw a towel over the remains; I'll clean it up later, red-hour-glass and all.

I tell you, Susan, don't you find it odd how one day I'm saving these eight legged creatures, and the next, pulverizing them with my sandal? Two totally different spectrums of life.

Am I God?

Lord help us!

Anywho, my point is I'm still not talking to you, or trying to make contact, even though I can't seem to break this habit of writing to you. I think it's because I don't have anything else to do. I'll just make sure you don't receive them until my last day here in Santa Fe, which is right around the corner.

I'll wait until I'm heading home before you'll ever know how much you hurt me.

You know the one thing keeping me going? It's those special moments you savor for the rest of your life.

I feel like I'm wasting my time, though, being here, trying to help you. Just a big fracking waste.

I can't wait until I'm done with you, until the day I don't have to think of you, worry about you, wonder about you! Will that day ever arrive? Soon, yes, very soon!

There are so many things I'd rather be doing right now than sitting in this god-forsaken backyard. Like lying on a beach somewhere, or sitting at a circus, even just riding a train from Detroit to Southfield. To be honest, I'd just about rather be doing anything else than what I'm doing right now.

I'm not, though, because I'm a man of my word, do you understand, Susan? I said I'd stay in Santa Fe, stay available to you until the end of the month. And that's only two weeks away. Then, then I'm outta here. Adios, sayonara. Hasta luego. See ya on the flip side. Gone.

You don't believe me?

Watch!

Just you watch!

Everything is quiet now, night-time sleeps in silence.

Your Friend,

Jack Monroe

Dear Susan,

I felt those little men racing around in my head again last night. I was kind of freaked out, because they'd been gone for so many days. I don't know what it is, could it be the microwaves floating in the air?

It's like they're all attached to a merry-go-round, and they run faster and faster and faster until my brain feels like mush.

I wonder if this is what it's like when a person starts to go crazy.

I'm studying the sky, clouds and such, and I see these planes whizzing by ejecting what I think is jet fumes. After a few minutes I notice the vapors begin to spread out over the vast blueness coating the atmosphere with what looks like a gassy cloud. I wonder what it is?

To me it looks like when the farmers get their fields sprayed.

Cropdusting!

I wonder what we're getting dusted with?

The little carnival men are gone. I can still feel the pressure of their tiny feet swarming around in my head. I can't believe they followed me to Santa Fe. I thought for sure I could shake them once I crossed the *Great Divide*.

Am I the sick one?

Did you know a duck's quack doesn't echo?

Now, that's a quack up!

Do you know what I think is one of the best flavor combinations?

White powdered sugar donuts and coffee!

There's nothing like the pallet tickler. I'm sure you've experienced the taste before and know exactly what I'm talking about. Huh! Huh! Am I right, Susan?

If you haven't, then you should. I know a great shop in Hazel Park where we can go.

It's located right down the block. We can walk. It's just this hole-in-the-wall diner called *Artie's*. He makes his own donuts. And man, oh man, are they good!

The dive is definitely what a greasy spoon is all about. Sometimes I wonder how he stays open, but then again his food is really tasty.

Maybe that's what I should do. Take some of my settlement money from the accident and open a small joint like Artie's. Or better yet, I should see if Artie wants to sell. That'd be great, don't you think, Susan? You can come work for me. And if you need a place to live, well, like I said before, my door is always open.

Don't you think life is much more exciting when you have plans?

When you make subtle changes to your everyday routine?

Change *is* good!

I can't remember the last time I talked to anyone, or saw someone up close. The rental apartment is getting messy again. I hate cleaning!

Sometimes living in this insane asylum of a world makes me nuts!

It's kind of funny in a way, how things feel like they've gotten out of control, and yet you haven't done anything.

Maybe that's why things feel so chaotic, because there's been no effort on your part to better your situation. You sit around whining and crying about how awful things are and that you only have two options, and yet refuse to opt for the medical choice. Who knows, maybe it won't be as bad as you think, you know, getting help from a neutral person. I don't know, Susan, something has to be done, because each and every day that passes, I begin to resent you more and more.

Don't tell me to *shut up*, you know how I hate that!

That's it, if you can't have any respect for me, I'm done talking to you.

Is today Sunday?

I hear the cathedral's bells tolling, and wonder if maybe I should go to church. Pray to my savior, whomever, or whatever that may be. I don't know anymore. Do you think I've misplaced my faith, Susan? Am I one of those lost lambs going off to slaughter? Do I not possess any saving graces? Am I vile and disgusting, and shouldn't be walking the face of this earth?

Am I nothing, if not a man?

Oh, Susan, I feel so foul, like my world is weakening. I see the first signs of dust floating in the air, as small cracks begin to crease my foundation. I'm like a cursed coal mine slowly caving in, rocks ricocheting off the crumbling walls while I bury the living deep beneath the ground.

I am lost!

Someone please help me. I don't know what is happening. It's as though I've taken on your depression, Susan, your sadness and despair, and I can't rid myself of it.

What's going on?

Was this your plan all along, Susan, to infect me with your hopelessness? Then maybe that'll make you feel better. Is this why you manipulated me into coming here, to Santa Fe, to stay holed up in this lifeless joint?

I hate you!

There, I said it. Are you happy? See what you've done to such a pure love as ours.

You've spoiled it, made it smell like rotten eggs. How dare you. Just who do you think you are?

I'll be glad when I'm finished with you once and for all!

Your Friend,
Jack Monroe

Dear Susan,

I'm not feeling any better, and I know I shouldn't be writing to you, but it seems to help with my moods. Plus, like I've told you before, you won't get these letters until I'm long gone.

The sky is rather beautiful with its robin egg blue, and misting clouds. I'm calmer, not as angry as I was in my last letter. I tell you, sometimes, I don't know what gets into me. You make me crazy!

Hey diddle, diddle, the cat and the fiddle, the cow jumped over the moon.

I'm beginning to understand why you want to commit suicide. Hell, right at this point in my life so do I!

Go figure!

Susan, do you think when it comes down to it, people really don't like themselves?

Did you know animals that lay eggs don't have belly-buttons?

I once knew a woman with no belly button, does that mean she lays eggs?

Yes, I'm just being silly. But you can see where I'm coming from, right?

Do you like being touched, Susan?

I don't!

I'm not sure why. But when a stranger touches me, it kind of creeps me out. Even when somebody I know touches me, my skin turns clammy and my body chills. It's a weird thing. I'm sure it has something to do with my childhood.

Doesn't everything?

Do you remember a program on TV a few years back where there was this woman who couldn't touch anyone because she would see their future, everyone she gazed upon seemed to have doomed fates. Do you think there is ever a happy ending for anyone?

To say the least, I thought the show was pretty interesting. Maybe I have something like that, but I can't see anything.

I'm just a freak. You can admit it out loud, Susan. I've known that about myself for quite some time now, and I've accepted it. It doesn't make me a bad person, though.

Am I being too harsh? My language too vulgar? I don't care anymore. I'm so tired of everything I'm beginning to realize how close I really am to jumping out of my window. What would my friends think when they came to see me? I wouldn't die, just break a few bones. Falling out of a one story building can't do that much harm.

I'd be an embarrassment to myself. If I'm going to go through the trouble of jumping out of something, I'm gonna make sure I kill myself, that's for sure. There's nothing more awful than trying to commit suicide and messing it up.

I sit here, Susan, looking out the window, listening to the rattle of a muffler-less car. It reminds me of an old man getting up in the morning, stiff and congested. He tries to loosen the dangling phlegm attached to the back of his throat, and hacks up a luggy.

I know, I know, you don't like it when I get gross like that. But once in a while it just comes out. After all, I am nothing but a man!

I hear children playing in the distance, their screeches and shrieks filter through my wall, my closed windows. I'm tempted to turn on my TV set, but then I'll get too engrossed in whatever is on, and I lose my concentration on you.

See, Susan, I'm still trying to contact you telepathically, again, since you refuse any physical contact. Can you hear me and will you listen to me?

There's something I want to tell you, Susan, something I think I figured out, but can only share with you in person. Don't let her hear us, or our plans. We have to remain very discreet, that's why my words have been so harsh, I'm trying to lead her off the trail. Make her think I'm abandoning you, and then we'll attack her after she lowers her defenses.

Susan, from this point on, we should only communicate with our minds, that way she won't know what's going on. I think she's been reading our letters.

Your Friend,
Jack Monroe

Dear Susan,

She tried to get in! You know, *that* crazy woman, your friend, Judith? She had a key—thought she could walk right in like she owned the place. Well, I surprised her. She didn't know about the deadbolt I'd just installed!

How'd she get a key?

Your Friend,
Jack Monroe

Dear Jack,

I finally installed the camera. I'll record my comings and goings for the next few days and then go from there. If this doesn't work, maybe I'll buy a hat camera and wear it all the time, that way I can see where she takes me.

I'm going to get to the bottom of this once and for all, and if there's nothing I can do, then I'll end it. My offer still stands Jack, about coming with me.

I'm a little tired, and there's a bunch of kids playing outside, kind of annoying me. My nerves are fried, and I wish I were dead!

Your Friend,
Susan Jordan

Dear Susan,

I'm still shaking from this morning when Judith came to the door. I, too, thought she was going to enter the apartment, until I recalled my foresight, and pulled the covers over my head. I was still in bed when this disturbance occurred.

The next time you see her, thank her for waking me from one of the deepest sleeps I've had in months.

Bitch!

Anywho, she pounded on the door a couple of times, and threatened to call the police if I—I mean you—didn't contact her.

They wouldn't do anything. It's not like you're missing. You just changed the lock on your door. That in itself is a sign you're alive. Which is good for me too, at least I know you haven't killed yourself yet.

Your friend finally gave up and left. I don't think we'll be hearing from her again.

Your Friend,
Jack Monroe

Dear Jack,

This afternoon I was in the backyard and heard a knock on my door. Peeking through a slit in the fence, I saw it was a cop. Sneaking upstairs, I lay on the floor of my work room, peering out the balcony window. I saw his car parked below. I froze! My breath caught in my throat like a hunk of un-chewed meat as he rapped a second time.

He glanced up toward my direction as he walked back to his patrol car. I ducked, hoping he didn't get a glimpse of my chestnut hair. Shaking uncontrollably, I crouched hidden on the carpeted floor.

I heard the cruiser pull away, and exhaled a stale breath. Shit!

Your Friend,
Susan Jordan

Dear Susan,

God-damn-it, I can't believe this. When I went downstairs, I found a camera in the living room. It was tucked away in a corner by the door. Has it always been there, did I not see it before?

No!

I would have noticed the intrusive device.

Oh, man, it's turned on. I don't understand; did the woman who lives here sneak in while I was sleeping and install a security system because she doesn't trust me? What have I done to warrant suspicion on myself?

Or, wait, could it have been *that* Judith woman? Maybe she paid someone to break in and spy on me. Could be bugs in the telephone.

I gotta get outta here!

Did you know a Kangaroo can jump thirty feet?

Your Friend,
Jack Monroe

Dear Susan,

I'm terrified. I think I might be losing my mind. Is this what happens in the *Land of Radiation*?

You know, Susan, sometimes I think about committing myself into an institution. Sit in a lounge chair all day, perched on a lush green lawn and look at nothing, think of nothing, do nothing.

I believe I've sunken into a deep depression again. I don't know why I say again, doesn't something have to stop before it can restart? Is that what's happening to us, we've stopped just so we can restart? Makes sense to me.

Come on, Susan, you seriously believe that? You really think people feel better after they've gotten into a fight with someone and then they make amends. Then again, as I sit here and think about it, you might be right. Maybe that's why some people are always causing havoc and drama in their lives.

So they can feel better about themselves.

Sometimes I wonder who's really the crazy one, me or society.

I'm contemplating cashing in my airplane ticket and taking a train to Detroit. I think riding the rails would be nice, take my time, try to decompress after all the emotional turmoil I've been through.

Do you want to join me?

Trains are great! They stream-line through desolate areas seldom seen by humans. Amtrak glides through wild forest pathways, racing with rushing rivers to the finish line, and then in a whisper, the Silver-Streak winds around a curve and suddenly is chugging through the depressed streets of a large city.

Talk about contrast!

Hey, Susan, I just had a brilliant idea. Why don't you take the express back with me and then we can both find a nice hospital to admit ourselves into? We can just relax together, you know, be around people who understand our turmoil. Someone who can take our feelings and help us sort them out. I'm sure we can find a nice institution for cheap, just as long as they let us be roommates, right? Otherwise, we might never see each other again.

We both know how those facilities can get.

What was that? You agree, it does sound like a good idea? Well, then, fine!

I'm so glad we're finally starting to see eye to eye. Life's been so hard lately knowing you might not want to have anything to do with me. I'm so happy I tried contacting you telepathically a second time. Who knew our minds would meld so quickly?

Your Friend,
Jack Monroe

Dear Susan,

I don't care, I took that damn Kodak down. Even if the woman who owns this place put it up, she should have contacted me about it first, after all, I still have till the end of the month, and there was nothing in our agreement about any spying.

Had it always been there? Are there others hidden around the apartment?

It would only make sense for her to have a system if she rents her place out to total strangers. I don't know anymore, Susan. I retrace my memories and can't see a camera in any of them.

I'm freaking out!

Maybe I should go for a walk.

Your Friend,
Jack Monroe

Dear Susan,

Glimmering windows reflect the descending sun, coating the mountains in blood. I watch the zealous moon rise over the evergreen tree line, slowly inching her way to the top of the sky. I can almost reach out and touch the creamy ball as it floats up to the heavens.

I feel innocent right now, void of any guilt or resentments, emptying myself of the green/yellow fungus living within. A purging of a lifetime, right here, right now. This is what I'm doing, Susan. We have to go in fresh this time, otherwise what has happened before will happen again.

Susan, do you think once a person stops seeing the beauty in life, they lose the desire to live?

Is that what has happened to you?

I can see how those kinds of things can easily occur these days.

I tell you, though, Susan, there's nothing like the beauty I'm experiencing right now. I wonder if you're seeing the same thing. Wouldn't that be cool!

Do you ever wonder why in only the past couple hundred years, humankind and technology have evolved at such an unbelievable rate? What was going on the rest of the time? Did someone discover a secret book that gave all the ideas away? I mean, come on, doesn't it seem fishy?

Why can't people think like this? Why does everything have to be so cut and dry, black and white, tit for tat? Will someone please explain this to me? I really, truly do not understand.

Susan, I need help!

Your Friend,
Jack Monroe

Dear Susan,

I didn't realize when we started communicating through our minds that you were such a chatter box. Do you ever shut up? I'm sorry, I don't mean to be rude, but you've been going on now for almost an hour nonstop about how you think there's someone else inside of you.

I know!

I know!

How many times do you have to tell me?

And if you remember, that's what we've been talking about all along, alien invasion.

We're their hosts.

What?

Hey, who are you to call me crazy?

Your Friend,
Jack Monroe

Dear Jack,

Enough with the mind talking, you're giving me a head-ache. I like you a lot more when I don't have to hear your voice.

Anywho!

I decided to take down the camera, it was kind of creep-ing me out, and when I watched it, all I saw was me coming and going. I don't know why I even bothered, I should have figured that's who I'd see. Maybe it's time for the baseball cap camera.

I *will* get to the bottom of this!

Your Friend,
Susan Jordan

Dear Susan,

I'm sicker than a dog. I don't know what happened, but I woke up in the middle of the night coughing up these black slugs, and blowing out this yellow thick snot. I've been in bed all day long, and just got up to write you. Now, I don't want you to worry about me, I'm sure this cold will pass in due time. I can't figure how I could have caught a bug, I haven't been out since the last time I went down to the plaza to meet you.

What a waste of time!

I guess the air is full of infecting spores flying all around us, invading our openings, settling in, and making us sick. I had the worst headache as I lay there in the dark. My heart was racing, my nose was dripping. I felt like hell.

Susan, can you imagine being sick all the time? I suppose there are some who do.

Cancer victims, aids patients, any kind of viral infestation. Don't you find it strange how there really wasn't a whole lot of cancer back in the middle-ages, or the nineteenth century, unless they just didn't make a lot of press about it.

That's why I believe our planet was invaded last century. The aliens live inside of us, making us sick, attacking our organs, latching onto our blood cells, changing us physically. Kind of like eating us alive from the inside out.

We shouldn't be worrying about the external invasion, because they've already invaded us internally.

Why not?

How farfetched could that really be?

I've heard a lot worse.

If you haven't guessed by now, I have a lot of theories. Most of them would be considered wacko by the average person. The only ones who don't think I'm nuts are those who think along the same lines as I do, and let me tell you, there aren't many. That's why I feel so lucky having found you, because we think so much alike.

Don't you agree, Susan?

Oh, how I love you.

Mist covers the mountains, drifting by the massive rock like shadows in a nightmare. I can see bronze beginning to tinge the leaves hanging tightly on the horse chestnut tree outside the window. The amber's western side is scorched scarlet, seared by the night-time's setting sun.

I'm better!

Sitting here writing to you opens my heart. My blood rushes through my body, surging me with energy, a lightness, as though I've purged myself of the devil. I know, though, he hasn't gone far!

Your Friend,
Jack Monroe

Dear Susan,

Listen to this poem I wrote, I don't know how, but it just came out. What do you think? It kind of scares me!

Farewell to Amarillo
Gunfire continues to echo
off uninhabited mountains,
though cease fire was
called for
time and time again.

Beaches once mauve
at sunset's peak,
now shadowed
by burnt black trees,
naked as though
winter was upon them.

Winds screech
through bullet holed branches.
I sneeze,
the air is full of white ash,
burning trash,
rot blends with smoke.

I see you scurry quickly
behind melted rock
demolished by missiles.
Your gun in hand,

finger on trigger,
posed to kill,
your body draped
in battle fatigues.

Your eyes flash
like a soldier
spotting enemy——
insane dullness.

I dive into the hole
I've dug for myself,
bullets fly relentlessly
above me.

They stop, I look up,
I hear your voice.
"Give up."
"Surrender."
"It's over."

I duck back down.
The air is cool again,
the island cast in fog.

This is how I feel!
Anywho!
Are you bored with me yet?
Yeah, me too. I'm tired of sitting here, day in and day

out, watching life walk outside my door, not delving into the experiences the world has to offer.

I don't want to be out there, though. It scares me. All those people milling around, not knowing who is whom, or what they are. Any minute you could be attacked, or spit upon.

Could be I'm getting tired of society.

Your Friend,
Jack Monroe

Dear Jack,

My nerves are wrecked!

I'm nothing but an echo in an empty alley!

I can't sleep anymore. Every time I lay down to rest, my mind begins to race out of control, spinning like a red and white striped top. I'm afraid it's a sign of her coming back and if I doze off she'll invade, so I jolt up and run around my apartment trying to keep the sandman at bay.

I don't know how much longer I can do this.

Your Friend,
Susan Jordan

Dear Susan,

It's so quiet right now in the middle of the night when everything slumbers. Sometimes, when I see someone, I wonder how they sleep. Is it restful and energetic, or tormented and disruptive? There are so many people with sleeping problems. I cannot help wondering if it's because there's so much electrical pollution.

I don't know. What I do know, though, is right now it is very quiet outside and inside.

That's all I have to say.

Your Friend,
Jack Monroe

Dear Susan,

Remember drive-in theaters? Golly, I loved them. Before Mom and Dad got weird with each other, we would go to the Galaxy Drive-In at least once a week during the summer. It was great! I'd lay out my sleeping bag in the back of Dad's yellow and brown Ford Custom station wagon—I think that's what it was called. It was like I was camping.

I was hot and bulky, as I'd wear my pajamas underneath my clothes. I didn't want to waste any time getting into my make-shift tent I had devised in the back of the car once the movie started. I didn't care how I looked. All that mattered was getting down to the playground area in front of the gigantic screen. My hand in Mom's, tugging at her arm, bidding her to go faster before the untangled swings were all taken.

I'd glance back at her as I broke her grip, her eyes fill with a sad joy. I could see tears welling in the half-mast lids. At the time I believed she was overcome with happiness, watching as her young boy played in the dusky sun.

Talk about a fond memory!

Last night I was watching this TV program. They were showing a man who'd been tarred and feathered. As he lay there dying, he saw himself when he was younger, poised on a pitcher's mound, doing what he loved best, playing baseball. The count was 3-2 with the bases loaded, up by one, two outs, bottom of the ninth. The manager strolls out to the mound, spitting black tar from his rotting mouth. He waves his puffy hand toward the bullpen, but the guy yanks it down, begging him to let him throw one more pitch. Reluctantly the coach retreats, and trots back to the dugout.

#9 takes his stance, nods at the signs, glances over his left shoulder to check on the runner. The wind-up, the pitch. *Strike*! The team rush at him, lifting him in the air, carrying his lanky body around the field as fans cheer in unexpected jubilation!

It makes me wonder, Susan, if at the point of death you see your most joyous moment?

I wonder what mine is, I've had so few!

No, I'm joking. I've had plenty; I just have to think of them.

Not to sound geeky, but I think one of them has to be when I met you!

That's just the most recent one I can think of.

My most joyous moment as a kid has to be when I was in grade school, sixth grade, I believe. It occurred during gym. We were playing basketball and I made two half court shots in a row. I was so proud of myself. Anyway, I ran home and rushed through the door, anxious to tell Dad, but he wasn't home. There was a note on the refrigerator door telling me my dinner was in the oven, and that he'd be home at nine. It would be hours before I could brag to him.

My disappointment sank deep in to the gray afternoon. The thrill I'd felt melted away, nothing seemed important any more. I choked my tepid turkey down, and went to bed. I never told Dad about my victory.

Maybe that was not the happiest moment of my life!

After that wonderful memory, I'll have to tap the well a little deeper to find another tantalizing tale. By the one and only, *Jack Monroe*!

Your buddy and friend to the end!

I can just be so silly at times, don't you think, Susan? But then what's life without a sense of humor?

I just got the taste of Bubble-Yum in my mouth. Grape! Remember the 70's, chewing gum molded like a strand? Multiple flavors lined the shelf; green apple, strawberry red, yellow banana. As soon as you tore open the wrapping, you could smell the sour sweetness of the candy.

How weird, to experience such a sensation after so many years!

Your Friend,
Jack Monroe

Dear Jack,

I'm frazzled!

The last straw has been drawn!

I have one more thing to do in this life, and then I'm out of here.

Why the immediate need to kill myself, you ask?

Well, let me tell you, Jack. This world sucks. It really does, not only to me, but to others. And to good people, Jack.

What am I talking about?

Well, if you'd stop interrupting me and let me finish, you just might find out.

Geeze, you're so pushy sometimes, I don't even know why I bother with you. You're not even man enough to respond to my requests and ideas. You know damn well what I'm talking about. Helping me get rid of the alias, and the other offer.

You know, sharing my journey with me?

Anyway, this morning the phone rang, startling me from a rare sleep. I thought I had turned it off.

Did you turn it back on?

No one left a message, and I was a little annoyed because it was only ten in the morning. Deciding to try and go back to sleep, it rang again, this time it was Judith. She wanted to let me know a mutual friend of ours just lost her eighteen-year-old son who had overdosed on heroin this past Friday night, and that the memorial would be Wednesday. Judith thinks it'll be nice if I can make it, and wants me to call her for more information.

Now how in the hell am I supposed to do that?

I can barely talk to you.

Will you call Judith, Jack?

Tell her I'm under the weather, and I'll talk to her when I feel better.

Please!

I will do anything for you, well, within reason.

If ever I needed you before, now is when I *really* need you.

Oh, what a tragic circumstance!

It should be me who is dead!

It should be you who is dead!

It should be us who are dead!

Your Friend,
Susan Jordan

Dear Susan,

I'm very dark today. Memories of Father's funeral reel through my mind like a 8 mm movie camera. Black and white, ticker-tape sounds clip the empty voices. Fuzz covers the tape, cracking and spitting out surreal images like one of Hitchcock's silent films.

I always got a creepy feeling when Dad would watch his old movies. Knowing all those people are dead, and yet there they were, preserved like media mummies.

Where'd you get that footage?

I felt nothing as they bull-dozed the dirt on top of his cheap coffin.

"What's the point in burying me in something expensive? It's just going to rot over time anyway, just like everything else does," Father would rant on whenever I mentioned anything about his arrangements and what he wanted done. He chose the dry-walled box himself!

Now, to me that's eerie. I don't want to know what I'm going to be buried in. As far as I'm concerned, you can chop me up into tiny pieces and scatter me around the forest to be eaten by the animals.

Because after all, aren't we all just food anyway?

Makes sense to me!

Your Friend,
Jack Monroe

Dear Jack,

Are you my assassin and I yours?

Is it your deadly intention to sidle up to me, get so close, so intimate that I can't even tell us apart anymore?

Whispering in my ear, "Don't do it, don't do it, there's so much to live for!"

Then, turning around and threatening me with your exodus from Santa Fe, retreating back to the dark/dank streets of down-on-it's-luck-Detroit.

I keep checking over my shoulder now, waiting to hear the sound of the safety snapping off, as the oiled trigger slips back like a gate closing shut.

Am I your assassin, and you mine?

Your Friend,
Susan Jordan

Dear Susan,

The weirdest thing happened to me, today. I went for a walk downtown, you know to get some fresh air. As I was strolling along the plaza I had this wonderful idea that I wanted to share with you, and I didn't want to forget it.

So, finding a pay phone, which isn't easy these days, I called the rental apartment to leave myself a message on the machine, but instead I got your voice mail. I dialed a second time, thinking I might've pushed the wrong number, but again, it was you. Maybe by accident I memorized your number, I'll have to check it when I get home.

Forgive me for the two hang-ups, it was me, but now I've forgotten what I wanted to tell you.

Your Friend,
Jack Monroe

Dear Susan,

Susan, when I checked the mail today, I found all of the letters I've written to you stuffed in the box. Did you send them back to me? I don't understand. You haven't opened one.

Confusion wracks my brain!

I'm so sick of you! All you are is a spoiled little brat who thinks she can say or do anything she wants to. Well, dear, you can't. I don't know why I even bother with you. It makes no sense to me. What was it about you that lured me into this self-destructive hell hole you call home.

I'm insane!

What else can it be?

I'm not attracted to you, and to be completely honest, right now, the thought of seeing you repulses me. You sniffling little self-absorbed liar. I don't think I could hate someone any more than what I feel for you right now.

I can't believe you!

You're so insensitive!

A coward!

That's what you are!

Well, you know what, Susan, I don't need you. It was you who needed me, and still do, but you won't admit it to yourself. I'm the one keeping you alive. Without me, you would have killed yourself long ago.

You know, Susan, usually I don't let people rattle me the way you have. I keep my distance, only doing casual things, never getting into the emotional side of a friendship, keeping everything cut and dry.

That's how I've avoided getting hurt all these years. That's how I've stayed single these past decades. That's how I've remained alone all this time. It's quite simple when you come right down to it.

What?

What was that you said?

You think I'm cold and cruel?

You think even though I put on the pretense I care, I really don't.

How can you speak those words after all I've done for you?

If there's been one person in your life who's been there through the thick and thin of your moods, your depressions, your threats, it's been me!

Don't you think I'm tired of it?

You know, Susan, a little thank you once in a while certainly can make a difference in one's attitude.

Your Friend,
Jack Monroe

Dear Susan,

Bright rays shine through the window turning my walls opaque. I hear the rasping caw of ravens bouncing off the adobe walls. Tar-black birds whoosh through the deep azure sky, blotting out the sun.

My horizons have shrunk, shriveled dry like a pitted prune. I can't do this anymore, to be perfectly honest.

I don't know if you can hear me or not, but I'm telling you, Susan, I'm becoming a dark day that will never see morning.

I guess you're beyond the point of caring how other people feel, or what you do to them. I can tell by your frigid responses. But don't worry, Susan, soon you won't have to deal with me at all, I promise.

Your Friend,
Jack Monroe

Dear Susan,

Sadness surrounds me, Susan. I don't know if I'm more-mad at you or myself. It's a fine line!

I've been crying for three days now after I discovered the unread letters.

I feel so empty inside, I can barely hear my heartbeat, the shattered organ pitter-patters against my hollow chest, like air-blown popcorn. Is this justified, has my life come down to these very few hours, minutes, seconds? Do I get a sixth of a second put back on the clock for good behavior?

Do you known children grow faster in the spring?

Your Friend,
Jack Monroe

Dear Jack,

I sit here sobbing, I'm so depressed, I can taste it, smell it, see the demon dancing in front of my eyes in happy jubilation.

I've lost, there's nothing to live for anymore. Everything is black and white, as though I've become color-blind. Will the red rose only be gray now, and the sky above, opaque? Grass of plaster beige cuts through my callused toes.

I have no inspiration, no desire to exist. See, Jack, little by little I die in front of me, the mirror is empty, the clichés are abundant, any originality has been twisted into the tornado, ripped apart and scattered millions of miles away.

Yet, I still hear beauty in music. Bach's *Air*, soothes my tormented soul.

Have I lived before, have I been alive forever, and just can't recall, or maybe I don't want to?

All I know is that I don't *want* to be here anymore.

Have you decided if you're coming with me or not?

Time is of the essence!

Your Friend,
Susan Jordan

Dear Susan,

This morning I was looking for your phone number to compare it to the number I dialed the other day. Instead, I came across an envelope of pictures. When I spilled them out onto the couch, I saw portraits of me and people I don't know.

I rummaged through them until I came to a still life of me and Judith. It seemed we were going to a party. Our arms were wrapped around each other, and by the looks of it, we are pretty chummy.

How could this be?

I don't even know the woman; she's your friend.

I'm a little freaked out right now, Susan. I'm not sure what to think.

Are things not what they seem?

By the way, I found the pills you left by the door last night. Please don't pressure me. Shouldn't the time be right for me, too? Shouldn't I be ready to cross the line to my destination? Right now I'm so confused I can't even recall my name.

Who am I?

Susan!

Jack!

Susan!

Jack!

Susan!

Jack!

Anywho are you?

See, my marbles are falling out of the bag.

Your Friend,
Jack Monroe

Dear Susan,

What are you trying to do?

I can see the implications you are making, especially now after I found the video you left in the bag with the pills.

I don't know what you're trying to do. Is this a little trick of yours? Deceitful and cunning as you are. I think you're up to something, and it's not in my best interest. I need to get out of town, at least out of this place before you show up to blow my head off.

See!

See!

See, Susan, see what you have done to me!

I don't know how you obtained this recording of me coming and going, going and coming, back and forth through your apartment. I've never even been there. It's not possible. What I'm going to do first thing in the morning is take the tape to some camera shop and see if they can tell if the cassette has been tampered with.

You're certainly going through a lot of effort to convince me that I might not be who I think I am. But hey, sister, you're wrong on that part. It's you who's having a problem coming to terms with your identity.

If it wasn't for me, you wouldn't even be around.

You're nuts!

I think all of the depressed days and nights have finally taken their toll, and you've lost any sense of reason. Is that it Susan?

I am not you!

You are not me!

We are two separate entities!

My gosh, what have I gotten myself into.

And now you propose I kill myself along with you. I'd have to be as crazy as you. But you must not be that whacked out if you devised this camera scheme. You really do look like me, but I guess we've always had a slight resemblance. I can see how Judith could mistake us.

Your Friend,
Jack Monroe

Dear Jack,

How dare you accuse me of plotting against you, trying to manipulate you into doing something your heart isn't into. Fine, if you don't want to continue this journey with me, go, just go. Return to your nothing life, in your nothing town, with your nothing thoughts. Because Jack, to be serious, you're nothing without me. You don't exist, you're just a figment of someone's imagination, and if you're not willing to do this, then I'll take you down with me!

And it won't be pretty.

I know who you are now; I too watched the recording!

Please, let's just end this peacefully!

Your Friend,
Susan Jordan

Dear Susan,

I came over to your house to return the pills you gave me. I'd decided I couldn't go through with it. I'm not ready to take my life, and I was hoping to talk to you in person, try to convince you not to go through with your plan.

When I arrived, there were lights and music on. *Winston*, I believe, *December*.

The air was eerie still and I smelled lilacs even though September draws to an end. My heart was light and free knowing at last I would confront you in person. I was both nervous and exultant as I knocked on the door.

No response!

Then again.

No response!

I whispered, "Hello!" Against the dirty brown wood.

No response!

Slipping around the corner to the nearest window, I peered through the hour glass of light and saw you lying on the Navaho blanketed couch, still as death. Finding a key in my pocket, I scurried back to the door, and surprisingly opened the lock without delay.

Stepping into the living room I warped out of time and found myself back at the apartment rental. How had I gotten here? Sense, common or not, grabbed hold of my mind and snuck the truth into my thoughts.

The flat must be Susan's. No wonder she was able to tape me. Oh, you, sly bitch! Look at you now though; dead, that's what you are, and you know what, I'm still here. Ha! I'm not going anywhere! Have fun on the other side without me, just see how long you last.

I went over to your chilling corpse and nudged your sallow shoulder.

No response!

"Susan," I mumbled, realizing I'd never spoken your name aloud before. The words felt hollow. "Susan!" I heard an echo.

She really did leave without me. I couldn't believe it. Was she running from me, trying to get away from I, who are her tormenter? Sadly, I do believe so. Maybe, just maybe though, I can catch up with her, and try to make amends.

The pills warm in my hand. They're so pretty. Little blue, pink, and yellow tablets waiting to take me to Never-Never-Land. I wish you could show me what it's like, since you're already there. Are the apricot blossoms in bloom, and the sky crystal blue? Can you smell fresh cut grass floating in the air, and feel a crisp breeze of late winter lick your/my brow?

Are you home?

Am I going home?

I'm not afraid, Susan, as long as I know you're waiting for me on the other side.

Your Friend,
Jack Monroe

Dear Jack,

The time has come!

The moment I found out who you are, I knew I had to bring you down with me, there are no two ways about it. Sure, I could have continued this way, going back and forth, forth and back, but to what point, Jack? There has to be an end to everything.

We would not have lasted much longer, they would have caught us, institutionalized us, subdued our demons with chemicals.

You deceived me, Jack, knowing who you are and yet continuing to disguise yourself as my friend and confidant, hoping all along that eventually I would fall and you would have full control.

I loathe you!

By the time you re-enter my mind, it'll be too late, the damage will already be done, and you won't be able to do anything about it. I'm sorry I had to go behind your back, Jack, but this is the best for the both of us.

Maybe if you would have been forthright from the beginning, things could have been different. Sneaking and scheming never pays off. Good luck wherever you end up Jack, and I pray our paths never meet again.

You *are* my assassin!

And I yours!

Your Friend,
Susan Jordan

Dear Susan,

There's an angle in the sky slicing clear through to heaven, spilling a sheet of rainbow through the dark storm filling the horizon. Lightning sparks in the background, white sun-streams glaze the mesas, turning the surrounding cliffs gold.

Is that where you disappeared to?

I'm feeling a little light-headed, the dope must be hitting me, soon I'll no longer be human, all that will be left of me is the shell of the man I used to be. What have I come to?

What a waste, don't you think, Susan?

You could have been!

I could have been!

We could have been!

Great!

Don't you think?

I had a right to exist just as much as you did, after all, it was you who created me, right? Made me an entity to help you? And now that I'm alive and fully kicking you want to rid your life of me.

That's not fair!

I will find you again, Susan, and when I do, I'll make everything right, you just watch and see. We're friends forever, don't forget that!

The angle in the sky has now closed its door, black stuffed clouds float above my eyes. I think I'll close them now and pray the carnival men stay away.

Anywho!

I have nothing against suicide, as long as it's for the right reasons!

Your Friend,
Jack Monroe

Dear Susan,

AUTHOR PHOTOGRAPH BY MARCELINO SILVA

Mary Maurice wrote her first poem when she was in the ninth grade, and hasn't stopped writing since. Catching the fire at an early age, she continues to dedicate her time to the craft.

Ms. Maurice has completed several novels of fiction and poetry, and has performed readings in distinct cities around the country. She presently resides in Santa Fe, New Mexico.